GREEN EYES IN

LAS VEGAS

A. R. WINTERS

Green Eyes in Las Vegas
Copyright 2014 by A. R. Winters

ISBN: 1499119313
ISBN 13: 9781499119312

—

Green Eyes In Las Vegas
(A Tiffany Black Story)

—

When cupcake-loving croupier and private investigator Tiffany Black witnesses a handsome, green-eyed man making a getaway after an art heist, she finds her normally chaotic life becoming even more complicated.

Tiffany flits between her two new cases — investigating the missing Van Gogh, and the murder of a Hollywood starlet with a secret life. When her investigation takes an intriguing turn and a man with mesmerising green eyes comes into her life, Tiffany starts to wonder if this man might be the missing link between both crimes.

As she follows the investigation from movie sets to museums, danger strikes a little too close to home when Tiffany discovers that not only was the murdered starlet being stalked, someone with a deadly motive appears to be watching her too...

ONE

I was walking down the street, minding my own business, when the man fell out of the sky.

He landed lightly on his feet and a parachute drifted to the ground behind him. I watched in silence as he unclipped the billowing fabric, bundled it neatly into a tiny roll that fit under his arm, and noticed me staring at him.

If I'd been thinking straight, I would have screamed.

But it was three o'clock on a Monday morning and I was standing on a deserted Vegas side-street. I'd left the bright, garish lights of the Strip behind me, and this street was as unexciting as it got – a tall apartment complex on one side, and the high, window-less wall of a small-time convention center on the other.

Anyone who reads the papers, watches the news, or is even vaguely aware of how the world works, knows that when a woman meets a strange man in a deserted side-street in the wee hours of the morning, he's more likely than not to be a thug, rapist, or murderer. Or all three.

But instead of screaming and running away, I stood there, frozen like a Greek statue, my mouth gaping, mesmerized by the man's gorgeous green eyes.

Sure, he *was* wearing a black ski-mask that covered the rest of his face. And yeah, he *had* just parachuted out of nowhere, wearing an expensive-looking black business suit, along with the ski-mask and parachute. If I'd been anywhere else, his strange dress-sense would've bothered me, but this was Vegas; I figured the man was just taking part in one of those high-adrenaline sports that are all the rage these days.

He winked at me, and I felt my knees turn to jelly. I stared as he turned around and walked up to a red Ferrari, parked half a block away. The view as he walked away was a feast for hungry eyes, but he reached the car all too quickly, stepped in and drove away.

I stood there by myself, still rooted to the spot, as the car disappeared over the horizon.

I've never been a fan of sappy rom-coms. I've always known that love and romance don't happen in real life the same way they do in the movies, and I'm cynical enough to know that no man could ever be half as perfect and charming and handsome as any of the leads in popular movies.

But I still stood there, on that deserted street, half-expecting Green Eyes to drive back and whisk me away with him. Or, at the very least, drive back and ask for my number.

After a while, when the street remained empty, common sense revisited me. I headed back home, replaying the events over and over in my mind. The way his eyes twinkled, the way he winked, the way he walked away so suavely.

The man was probably just another visitor to Vegas, someone who'd be on a flight back home in a couple of hours. Most likely, I'd never see him again. But that didn't stop me from creating a fantasy life for the two of us as I trudged home…

TWO

It was almost four when I reached my tiny condo and after a long night of dealing cards to hopeful gamblers, I could barely keep my eyes open.

I dumped my mail on the coffee table, where it joined a growing pile, and glanced at the dying cyclamen that was sitting in a pot on my kitchen windowsill. The place needed a vacuum and the kitchen needed a mop, but that would have to wait. It also needed some artwork on the walls, decent curtains and a light bulb needed changing – but all those things would have to wait, too. I was exhausted.

I'd purchased my condo with my own meager savings a few months back, thanks to the collapsing Vegas real estate market. The building is run-down, with the Home Owner's Association unable to raise fees for proper security guards or a fancy pool area, but that suits me fine. It's within walking distance of the Strip, my friend Glenn lives downstairs, and hopefully I'll move somewhere nicer as soon as I can afford to.

I was asleep within minutes of my head hitting the pillow, and the next thing I knew, light was streaming in through my bedroom window and my cell phone was buzzing.

I reached out to switch it off, but relented and groggily answered when I noticed the caller ID, wondering what the hell was going on.

"Hi, Tiffany!" Emily Sinclair sounded annoyingly alert. "I didn't wake you up, did I? Wasn't yesterday your day off?"

"No," I grumbled, trying my best to sound coherent. "I had to go in after all. But it's fine, I'm up now."

"Oh…" Emily paused. "How are you?"

"Same as last week. Still between cases."

I'd just become an accredited private investigator in the hope of being able to quit my job at the casino, and on my very first case, I'd uncovered the person behind multi-millionaire Ethan Becker's murder. Although this early success had infused me with more cockiness than I deserved, and some deep-rooted hopefulness, it didn't mean that clients were lining up around the block to hire me. Yet. I was still crossing my fingers and hoping for the best.

A quick glance at the clock showed me that it was almost twelve, so Emily was probably taking an early lunch break. Her work as an LVMPD detective was pretty stressful and, although we were reasonably good friends, she wouldn't be calling in the middle of the day unless there was something important she wanted to talk about.

"I'm sure something'll come up," she said. "But right now I'm dying to know – how was the dinner?"

I frowned and rubbed my eyes, and then I remembered. "Right." I'd completely forgotten to update Emily. "Did Nick tell you anything?"

"I asked him how it went and he shrugged and said something like 'Mehhrghw.'"

I laughed. "Yeah, that sums it up. Maybe we'll stay friends, but it's not going to be romantic."

"Bleh." Emily sounded disappointed and I felt a quick pang of guilt. After all, she was the one who'd set us up, and Nick was her co-worker, so things might be awkward for her. But was it my fault the chemistry wasn't there?

"He was a bit boring," I said.

"He's cute, he's funny and he's a nice guy. Nice guys don't just fall from the sky."

I smiled to myself. "Actually…"

"What? You've met someone else?"

I sighed. "Not quite." I found myself telling Emily the whole story, ending with Green Eyes' driving away.

She was silent for a few long seconds after I'd finished my tale, and then she said, "Tiff. You've got to come into the station and make a statement."

I laughed nervously. "So, now it's a crime to see a man jumping off a building?"

"No. But the street where you saw this guy…It was the little side street just off The Cosmo Hotel, wasn't it?"

"Yea-eah." I was awake enough to recognize the heavy feeling in the pit of my stomach.

"I'm pretty sure the guy leaped off Ascend Towers."

"So?"

"We just had a burglary report. Someone stole a Van Gogh from the Ascend Towers penthouse."

—⁓—

I WAS ON hold briefly while Erika transferred me to Detective Elwood, who she said was working the Ascend burglary. While I waited, I remembered my view of the man walking away, and the heavy feeling in my stomach got worse. In addition to the bundled-up parachute under his arm, he'd also had a narrow poster tube slung across his back.

"Yeah."

Elwood's gruff voice startled me and I sputtered, "Uh, huh-hello. This is Tiffany Bl-"

"Yeah. Sinclair says you witnessed something."

I rolled my eyes. The man had the raspy voice of a two-pack-a-day smoker and the condescending tone of a man who knew everything.

"Yes," I said. "I saw a man jumping off a building on Cecil Stree-"

"Did you actually see him jump out?"

"No, I heard a noise behind me and turned around just in time to see him land. He-"

"But you didn't see him actually jump?"

"No, I-"

"Was he behaving suspiciously in any way?"

The man's interruptions annoyed me, but I thought back to Green Eyes' behavior. He'd winked at me, but surely that wasn't too suspicious? Surely an attractive man might want to wink at me. "I guess not."

"Then what makes you think he's tied up with the burglary?"

"I don't – I mean – maybe he's not." I didn't *want* to believe that Green Eyes was involved in anything illegal; I'd much rather think of him as a thrill-seeking urban-sports lover.

"Then why was Sinclair dumb enough to think I'd want to talk to you?"

I felt a flash of loyalty toward Emily, sucked in my breath, and spoke quickly so Elwood couldn't interrupt me. "He was wearing a ski-mask and carrying a poster tube and a parachute."

Elwood was silent for a second and then he said, "Come into the station to make the report. Can you make it within the hour?"

"Yeah," I felt my heart sink. I didn't really want to talk to Elwood or get involved in this, but I didn't see how I could say no.

"Good."

He hung up before I could say anything else, and I cursed myself silently, hoping that Green Eyes wasn't really involved in anything illegal.

THREE

Whooshing out the door soon after waking up is not my idea of how the day should start.

I grumbled to myself about cops who had nothing better to do than rush me out of my own home, and people who never let me finish my sentences. I tried to tame my frizzy brown hair and gave up quickly, pulling it into a low ponytail. Autumn had kicked in, and the temperature wasn't meant to go beyond eighty today, so I found a clean pair of black slacks and a green top to wear. Stilettos seemed too fancy for a quick visit to the police station, so I settled for sensible black ballet flats, grabbed my all-purpose big tote, and headed out the door.

I steered my beat-up old Accord toward the police station, avoiding the stupid tourists on the road who didn't know how to drive, and a niggling doubt bothered me – had Elwood criticized Emily on purpose, just to make sure I told him everything I knew?

Once I reached the station, I waited only a few minutes before I was ushered through the modern, sterile halls to the open area where Elwood's desk was. The moment I saw him, I realized there was no way he was smart enough to have tricked me into revealing what I knew – he was a chubby, grumpy figure of a man, slumped over his desk with some paperwork. Stubble covered most of his face, and the visible rest was contorted into what seemed like a permanent grimace. One hand gripped a large, white coffee mug, and when he noticed me and looked up, I saw that he was squinting with annoyance.

Elwood looked exceptionally displeased to see me. He nodded toward the chair in front of him, and as I sat down, he took another sip of his coffee. It looked weak and watery, and judging from the rolls of fat that hung off his neck, I guessed that his drink contained more cream and sugar than caffeine.

"Tiffany Black?"

"Yes."

"So you decided to show up?"

He made a big show of looking at his watch and I stifled a grimace. "I'm only five minutes late. Traffic was crazy a—"

"Oh no, that's fine." His voice was laced with sarcasm. He spread his hands wide apart, and I noticed the gold wedding band on one of his pudgy fingers. "I'm happy you made it at all. I know how you women like to make a late entrance. My ex-wife was the same, always running late when we had to go somewhere."

"Oh." I shifted uncomfortably, wondering what to say.

"So, tell me what you saw." He smiled at me, like he was indulging a toddler who claimed to have seen a unicorn. "Where were you? What time?"

"Three a.m.," I said, and tried to describe the location as best I could.

"What were you doing there at three?"

"Walking home from work."

"Oh?"

It was clear that despite my conservative outfit, he thought I was one of Vegas' many prostitutes, so I quickly added, "I'm a dealer at The Treasury Casino."

"Huh." He narrowed his eyes and looked at me carefully. "My ex is a dealer, too. You know, you even look a bit like her. Same kind of hair, same cunning eyes."

This conversation was getting a bit awkward. I'd never heard anyone describe my eyes as cunning before, and before I knew it, I was saying, "When did you get divorced?" Elwood narrowed his eyes and I quickly said, "Right. Never mind. As I was saying…" *What was I saying?*

"Two months," Elwood said. "She'll change her mind in a bit, she's always changing her mind on stuff. That's why I still wear my ring. Women, huh?"

"Yeah, women," I said. I nodded my head and tried to sound as though I, too, found all women exasperating and fickle.

His eyes shone and he leaned forward. "You say something they don't like, they pitch a fit. What'm I meant to do, stand there quietly like some whipped loser?"

"Uh-hunh," I said, nodding slowly. "Exactly."

Maybe my voice had a hint of sarcasm that I couldn't disguise, or maybe some pity showed through eyes. Either way, Elwood leaned back and seemed to remember that he didn't want to talk to me. He took a dejected sip of his sugary coffee, and tapped his pen awkwardly.

"So, this guy?"

I repeated the story of Green Eyes' Earth landing once more, my words coming out in a rush. Now that I knew about the former Mrs. Elwood, all I could see sitting in front of me was a tiny, sad man covered in layers of cookie dough. It wasn't pleasant – kind of like seeing a naked bogeyman.

Elwood listened blankly, not asking any questions, until I was done talking.

"So, that's it," I finished lamely. "I guess I should get going."

"Sure."

We exchanged awkward goodbyes; Elwood seemed as relieved as I that our chat was over, and I headed out, wondering if what I'd seen would even contribute to the burglary investigation in any way. He hadn't seemed to take what I'd said very seriously, and other than getting to hear some wisdom about women, I felt like my time had been wasted.

I was about to leave the parking lot when my phone buzzed.

FOUR

"Tiffany Black?" I hadn't recognized the number, and now I didn't recognize the voice. It was female, deep and smooth: clearly the voice of someone who was used to being listened to. "My name's Samantha Sanders. Sophia told me about you?"

I smiled involuntarily, my eyes seeing dollar bills before me.

Sophia was my first – and so far last – client. An ex-stripper turned casino-owner's wife, turned casino-owner's widow, she'd been accused of killing her husband. After I managed to prove her innocence, she promised to refer me to people she knew. I'd been waiting for one of her wealthy buddies to give me a call, and hopefully hire me to do some easy, well-paying work.

And now here I was, speaking to Samantha. I mentally took back all the grumbling I'd done about Sophia forgetting me.

"Sophia spoke really well of you," Samantha was saying, "and I'd like to hire you for some work. It's a bit urgent – can you come chat with me today?"

"Of course." I had nothing planned for today, and I knew these high-powered types were always busy. "I can come over straight away."

"Great."

I was expecting Samantha to ask me to come over to her office, so I was a bit surprised when she gave me the name and address of a diner in a slightly sketchy part of town.

"Are you sure?" I asked. "I can always come over and meet you at work."

There was a brief pause as Samantha considered that option, and then she said, "No, work might be a bit awkward."

I wondered if she wanted me to look into one of her employees. And then an unnerving thought struck me. I said, "How do you and Sophia know each other?"

"We used to work together."

I stifled my groan. It was just my luck. They weren't opera-buddies, or co-members of some charity board. "Oh."

I must've sounded disappointed because Samantha immediately said, "You don't have to do the work if you don't want to."

"No, I do. I mean, I don't know yet, but I'll come and talk to you."

"Ok, I'll see you in a few minutes."

I hung up and as I drove over, I remembered working for Sophia. It hadn't been much fun. Early in my investigation, I'd been backroomed in The Riverbelle Casino by two goons who had more brawn than brains. Mr. Beard had been bald, with a French cut beard, and Beady Eyes had, well, tiny beady eyes. They seemed to want to hurt me for fun and, in the end, I'd only managed to escape by slipping off the stiletto I'd been wearing and driving the pointy end through the side of Mr. Beard's neck. I hoped nothing like that would happen if I decided to accept Samantha's case.

Neil's Diner was a little bit west of the Strip and two doors down from The Peacock Bar, where Samantha worked. While The Peacock Bar catered to well-heeled locals and curious tourists, Neil's Diner seemed to cater exclusively to employees of the bar, and a few well-informed locals who went there to ogle at the girls for the price of a cheap, greasy meal. It was a badly-lit place that seemed to have been set up sometime in the fifties, with the same, decades-old dirty red booths lining one wall, and a few rickety plastic-and-chrome tables and chairs in the middle of the room.

Within seconds of walking in, Samantha waved me over to one of the booths with high-backed, uncomfortable red seats. I'd told her to recognize me by my outfit, but I needn't have bothered – I was the only woman there who didn't have the face of a supermodel or the body of someone familiar with plastic surgery.

Samantha was a brown-eyed brunette with a friendly smile. She wore a pink singlet and tiny denim shorts, a stark contrast to the dark business suit I'd been picturing her wearing for the first few minutes of our phone conversation. As I slid into the booth, she said, "Thanks for coming over."

I mumbled something polite, trying to forget that I'd initially thought she was a powerful executive or casino owner's wife.

"I know you're busy," Samantha said. "Sophia said your name was in the papers after you solved Ethan Becker's murder, and you must have lots of clients."

I let the comment slide, not wanting to acknowledge how desperate I was for a new client. My work as a casino dealer pays the bills, but I'd love to get out of the fickle gambling industry and do more meaningful work.

"I'm so glad Sophia told me about you," she went on. "I don't know who else to go to, or who to trust."

Samantha looked at me with large, pleading eyes, and I felt a prickle of worry. A simple case shouldn't involve much skill or trust…"What's this about?"

Samantha pulled up a photo on her phone and slid it over to me. It had obviously been taken recently, because she still had the same hairstyle. She was standing next to a gorgeous blonde, and they were both posing for the camera, hands on their hips, red carpet style.

I clutched at a straw of hope. "You want me to follow this blonde?"

"Not much of a psychic, are you? That's Crystal. She died four days ago."

"Oh. I'm sorry to hear that. Was she…?"

I let my voice trail off and Samantha sighed. "The police said it was mugging gone bad. She was stabbed in a street in North Vegas, just past Aliente."

Aliente was a newish, northern suburb, near where my parents live. "So the police looked into it. I'm sorry for your loss, but if they've already investigated, I don't think there's anything I can do."

"No." Samantha shook her head emphatically. "You've got to help out. I couldn't tell the cops everything."

I leaned forward, and rested my chin on my hands. I wasn't looking forward to diving into another murder investigation and I didn't like the idea of keeping information from the cops.

I stared at Samantha until she sighed again and went on. "Crystal was a stripper, just like me. Nobody knows that – not her sister, not her boyfriend."

I looked at her sympathetically. "I understand, but right now - maybe it's time to let the cat out of the bag."

Samantha shook her head again. "She didn't want anyone to know and I don't want to betray her, especially now that... Anyway, I'm sure being a stripper had nothing to do with it."

"Maybe not. But maybe it did."

"I can't take the risk – her family back home are conservative and I don't want...I couldn't do that to her, or their memory of her."

As messed up as it was, I could understand Samantha's point. "Ok," I said, "tell me what happened."

"As far as I know, Crystal went out one night. I'm not sure what she was doing up in Aliente, but the next morning, her boyfriend Max called to see if she was with me. She wasn't, and she wasn't answering her phone – and then the cops called me and told me her body had been found."

Samantha blinked back tears and I reached out instinctively and squeezed her arm. After a few seconds I said, "Why were the cops calling you?"

"I'm listed as her emergency contact here." Samantha smiled wryly. "She was my flat-mate, which is the only reason I even know about it."

I waited for her to blink away the tears that welled up again. A petite, blonde waitress in a faded red-and-green uniform appeared with a drink Samantha must've ordered earlier, and asked me if I'd like anything to eat. As if on cue, my stomach rumbled, and I remembered I'd skipped lunch. I ordered a chicken burger, and Samantha said, "I wish I could eat carbs."

I smiled. "Anyone can eat carbs. You just need to be ok with a bit of chubbiness."

"Or a gym membership."

Or dancing around a pole all day. Or standing on your feet all night long, dealing out cards to annoying, drunk strangers. But I didn't mention either of those options out loud.

Instead, I said, "If Crystal's friends and family don't know she's a stripper, what do they think she does?"

Samantha took a long sip of her drink. "Crystal doesn't live here – *didn't* live here. She lives up in LA, where she's – she was – trying to be an actress. She flew down once a month to work at The Peacock, and told everyone she was doing modeling work at conventions."

I nodded. "That's why she flew down this weekend."

"No. This time Crystal flew over for the Indie Movie Convention, and she stayed back because she thought she might get a role in Casino Kings. That's a movie being shot here," she added.

"Right. So she was staying with you?"

"No. Her boyfriend came down with her, and they were staying in The Palazzo."

My run as a psychic was going from bad to worse, so I said, "Her boyfriend doesn't know she's a stripper?"

"No way. He's the jealous type."

I couldn't imagine keeping such a big secret in a relationship, but it seemed like no biggie to Samantha. "Were they serious?"

She shrugged. "Maybe he was serious about her. They've been together almost three years – I assumed she'd work it out with him at some point."

I nodded like I understood, but I didn't really. The waitress came by with my burger, and for a few long seconds the only sound was that of my chomping and chewing.

My phone rang when I was half-way through my burger. It was just my mother, so I ignored it and put it away. I looked at Samantha and asked, "Why talk to me? I mean, what makes you think this is anything beyond a mugging gone bad?"

Samantha toyed with a strand of her hair. "Crystal was wearing a massive diamond ring that night. She was still wearing it when she was found."

"Did they take anything from her at all?"

"Yeah…her purse was empty, so they took whatever cash she had, and her phone."

"Maybe they panicked and forgot the ring."

"That's what the cops said. But I think…" She shook her head. "It's just this feeling I've got, that there's something more…Crystal was like a sister to me, and I need to do this for her. She'd have done the same for me. Please say you'll look into it?" I swallowed my mouthful and was about to say something when she added, "I'll pay whatever you want."

I nodded thoughtfully and finished up my burger. A new client who'd pay well was nothing to sneeze at. And my gut agreed with Samantha – there did seem to be something fishy about the whole thing.

"I can't guarantee anything," I said.

"But you'll look into it?"

I nodded, yes, and Samantha let out a deep breath and smiled. I pulled out a copy of my PI contract, which I always carried in my bag, and we went over the paperwork. Once everything was complete, Samantha began typing into her phone and said, "I'm emailing you those photos of Crystal."

I nodded, and rummaged in my bag until I found a notebook and pen for taking notes.

"I'll need more info on Crystal," I said. "Let's start with the basics – what can you tell me about her?"

Samantha thought for a moment, and then began reeling off facts about Crystal. Her real name was Crystal Macombe, her stripper name was also Crystal. She'd grown up in Nebraska; both her parents had passed away but her sister, Carol, still lived there. Carol was married with three kids. Crystal had always wanted to be a movie star and Samantha thought she was gorgeous and talented.

"What about the boyfriend?" I asked.

"Max works in finance, I think he earns a fair bit. He's pretty shook up about the whole thing, and as far as I know, he's still in Vegas."

"I guess I should talk to him."

Samantha nodded. "Yeah, he might be helpful."

"Have you told him you're hiring a PI?"

"Yeah. He's not thrilled about the idea, I think he just wants to move on. But I think he'll help us – hang on."

Samantha pulled out her phone and I watched as she called Max and began explaining that she'd hired a PI. As I listened, I thought about Max's reticence to investigate and remembered the old police cliché of "it's usually the husband."

"Ask if we can come over now to talk to him," I prompted Samantha. I wasn't sure how long Max would stay in Vegas, and I didn't want to miss an opportunity for a face-to-face chat.

After a few minutes, Samantha hung up and turned to me. "He said he'll help out as much as he can."

I nodded, and took a few seconds to look over my notes. "What did the cops say?"

"Not much. They think she was mugged, and she was stabbed twice, most likely by one person."

I had a few more questions, but I figured I should ask them while Max was also there. "Why don't you come with me when I go to see Max?"

Samantha nodded, settled the bill, and walked with me to the parking lot. I got into my '99 Accord, and she stepped into a brand-new red convertible.

After I watched her drive away, I called my mother.

"Tiffany Black!" she said as soon as she picked up. "*What* are you doing in Neil's Diner? You're not – you're not looking for work nearby, are you?"

I rolled my eyes. "What makes you think I'm in Neil's?"

"Your nanna's friend's brother, Louie, saw you walk in. What's going on?"

I sighed. Nanna had moved to Vegas ten years ago to live with my parents, and though she's not a local, she quickly infiltrated Vegas' Mafia-like Old People's Gang. She and her friends are never up to any good, and seem to know every other person who lives here. A rumor can never die safely with them around.

"I'm just talking to a new client," I told my mother.

"For PI work?" she asked suspiciously, and I sighed.

"Yes. For PI work. What other kind of work would I do?"

"I don't want to even think about that," my mother said. "Why can't you just get a regular job, where you don't have to walk into places like Neil's Diner?"

"Neil's Diner isn't so bad," I told her. "And I have to go now, I'm late for a meeting."

I hung up before she could say anything else that would remind me of how big a disappointment I was to her, and headed over to The Palazzo, where Crystal's boyfriend Max was staying.

FIVE

Maxwell Gomez was not what I'd expected. He was stocky, balding and obviously distressed about Crystal's death.

"I shouldn't have let her go out that night," he told us. "I asked her if I should go with her, but she said it was a work party and I'd be bored."

He sat miserably on the edge of the hotel sofa, head resting on one hand. We were sitting in the "living" area of his Palazzo VIP suite, with its cream leather sofas and bright abstract artwork. At my request, Max had given us a quick tour; the place was larger than my condo, obviously much cleaner and came complete with in-room hot-tub and gorgeous views down the Strip.

"Maybe we shouldn't have come down here," he continued. "But it was our three year anniversary, and I wanted to do something nice for her."

And he had, I thought, trying not to feel jealous. In addition to the massive suite, I was pretty sure he'd also been shelling out for fancy dinners and shows, and probably a nice gift or two.

"That reminds me," I said. "Samantha told me you'd given Crystal a diamond ring she wore that night."

"Yes." He got up, and retrieved the ring from a box nearby. "The cops kept it in evidence for a bit, but they gave it back to me because they think the case is solved. Speaking of which," he glanced from me to Samantha, "I don't know about this PI stuff. I mean, it's hard enough to accept that she's gone. I don't – don't like the idea of –"

He paused, unable to find the right words, but I knew what he meant. He wanted to accept the closure provided by the cops, grieve and move on with life. At least, I thought that's what he meant.

Samantha nodded sympathetically, and said, "Honey, we all want to put this horrible thing behind us. But what if the cops were wrong? I owe it to Crystal to do this. I know you understand…"

Max sighed. "I guess you're right." He turned to me and said, "What did you want to ask?"

"Well, for starters, how long are you in Vegas for?"

"Till Friday. I've also got meetings with local clients till the weekend."

"What do you do?"

"I'm a quant at CBN Investments."

I looked at him, puzzled, and Max began explaining his work to me eagerly – something about neural networks and deltas and investments. It didn't make much sense, but I made my "Ah! Now I get it!" face and smiled and nodded.

When he was done explaining, I turned my attention back to the ring he'd given me. It was an anniversary band, white gold and studded with diamonds all the way around. Whatever his job was, clearly it involved earning lots of money.

"Tell me about Crystal," I said. "What was she like?"

Max's face transformed into a dreamy reverie. "She's wonderful. Beautiful and kind and funny. Generous. Smart. I never thought she'd go for a guy like me – she's gorgeous enough to have any guy in the world, but she picked me."

"Why do you think that was?"

Max shrugged. "I was good to her, I guess. I supported her, loved her – I gave her anything she wanted. But any guy would do that for a woman like Crystal. I guess I was just lucky."

He sighed deeply, and I wondered how much of their relationship was based on him giving her "anything she wanted." It was tempting to ask him what he got her for her last birthday, but instead, I said, "I hate to ask this, but was Crystal…did you ever suspect any other guy of being with her?"

Max laughed. "This is Hollywood we're talking about. Every other guy hit on Crystal, some sleazy director or screenwriter was always thinking she'd sleep with them."

"And did she?"

He shook his head, no. "I would've known. And I think she would've just broken up with me, instead of cheating on me. I get a bit jealous sometimes, but she had standards. Morals. A lotta guys offered to get her roles in movies, but she always said no. She was ambitious; she wanted to do it all herself, the right way." He looked at me, his eyes shining with belief. "There was no-one else."

I glanced at Samantha, who was looking intently out the window. "What about enemies? Was there anyone who might want to hurt her?"

"No, she was a sweetheart. Always got along with everyone." He paused for a moment and frowned. "Unless that stalker thing wasn't a joke."

Samantha turned around and we exchanged glances. She said, "What stalker thing?"

Max said, "She never said anything to you?" He got up, walked over to the desk and sorted through some paperwork. "Here."

He handed me an envelope, and I opened it to find stacks of photos. Crystal talking with some other girls, Crystal doing her grocery shopping, Crystal looking over her shoulder.

I frowned. "What're these?"

Max turned to Samantha and asked, "Crystal never told you anything about the stalker?"

Samantha looked as puzzled as I felt and shook her head.

"She got these in the mail. I asked her what was going on, but she just laughed and said a friend of hers was being funny and pretending to be a stalker. Pretending like she was a big movie star. It was a joke, she said."

I turned one photo over. There was nothing on the back. "Did she seem upset?" I asked.

"No. She found it funny."

I passed the photos over to Samantha who looked at a few and shook her head. "No. Crystal never said anything about a stalker."

"I wonder..." Max paused. "Do you think she was just trying to make me feel better by saying it was a joke? These photos look pretty...stalkerish."

We were all looking at the photos thinking the same thing: if someone was really stalking Crystal, maybe this person had also killed her. And if they hadn't killed her, but were watching, maybe they'd seen who had.

SIX

I squinted at one of the photos. "Where was this taken?"

Max went through the photos slowly. "All of them were taken here in Vegas."

"Did anyone know about the stalker?"

He shook his head again, looking helplessly at Samantha. "I thought you were Crystal's best friend. If she didn't mention it to you, I don't think she told anyone else."

"He's right," Samantha told me. "She didn't tell me anything. Either it wasn't important enough to her, or she was keeping it secret."

I nodded, and gathered up the photos.

"What about her work?" I asked. "What was Crystal doing here?"

Samantha had already told me, but I wanted to see if Max's version of the story matched up with Samantha's. It did, and I listened while Max told me all about how Crystal was trying to make contacts at the Indie Movie Convention, and how the role in Casino Kings might've been her big break.

"Did she have any other friends in Vegas? Maybe other actors at the convention, or working in Casino Kings?"

Max frowned. "She did talk to me about work, but I can't remember names. She was pretty close with this one girl who worked on the set...Maggie, Marjory, Macey-"

"Minnie," said Samantha. "She's a makeup artist on set."

"How come they're already shooting the movie?" I asked. "I thought roles were always decided ages in advance?"

"It's an indie movie," Max said. "Low-budget, but expected to win some prizes. Crystal would've gotten a side-role. Sally Herbert was meant to play it, but she got sick, so they needed a quick replacement. Crystal was all set to be it."

I frowned. "Do you think someone might've been jealous that Crystal got the role?"

Max shook his head. "It wasn't a done deal, but she'd probably have signed on in a few days. I'm not sure who would be jealous – it was just a supporting role in an indie move. Though Crystal had high hopes."

"But you never know with these Hollywood types," Samantha added, and I agreed. Not that I knew any Hollywood types in person – but what little I'd seen in *OK!* and *People* made me think they weren't very nice people. Although the role didn't sound like much to kill for.

"Anyway," Max said, getting up and walking over to the desk again, "These are her papers. Mail and stuff – in case it helps."

"Thanks." I was a little surprised by how organized he was, but pleased that he'd put the papers aside for me. As I shoved them into my purse, I wondered if his helpfulness was genuine. Had he sorted through the papers since we'd called, putting away something that might incriminate him? Was his naïve, heart-on-sleeve misery just a big act?

Looking at him, I found it hard to believe he'd ever yell at a person, let alone kill them. But I still asked, "Did you and Crystal have any fights recently? Any major disagreements?"

He shook his head. "We never fought. If I disagreed with her, it was always about something minor, so I let it pass."

Whipped, I thought, and tried not to smirk; I groaned, and tried to get Elwood's voice out of my head.

Samantha and Max both stared at me.

"What's wrong?" Samantha said.

Max looked concerned. "Was it a bad thing we never fought? Should I have disagreed with her more often? Some people say you need to fight to keep a relationship healthy, but I never saw it that way."

"Nothing's wrong," I said, staring at Max, and tried to stop the voice inside my head from making a reappearance. "Umm… did Crystal seem any different recently? Stressed? Afraid?"

Max and Samantha both shook their heads. "No," Max said, "If anything, she was more upbeat than ever, because she thought she was getting her big break."

"Yeah," said Samantha, "she said this might be her last time coming down to Vegas."

"And she wasn't always running around anymore," Max added. "She used to spend all her time updating social media, trying to get in touch with people, making phone calls and texting. But the day before she died, we spent the whole day together. Didn't even leave the hotel – just hung out in the spa, spent time together, relaxed. I can't believe…" He shook his head. "I just can't believe it."

I nodded, trying to think of things I might be overlooking. "What about her family?" I asked. "Was it just her sister?"

"Yeah," said Max. "Christine. She's a couple years older than Crystal, married to her high school sweetheart and lives out in Nebraska – Crystal and I visit go see her on holidays."

I nodded. "And did they get along?"

Max shrugged. "They weren't besties, but Crystal told me they grew closer after their mom died a few years ago. Their dad died when they were teenagers."

"Any other family? Uncles and aunts, cousins?"

"A handful – but they don't live in Nebraska or the West Coast, so I've never met them. I know Crystal adored her sister and little nieces and nephews, but she didn't want her sister ever coming to Vegas, just in case…"

"How 'bout you? Did you and Christine get along?"

Max shrugged again. "Decently enough. She's pretty conservative. And she wanted to have the funeral in Nebraska, but of course that's not possible – all Crystal's friends are in LA."

I turned to Samantha and said, "Did you ever meet Christine? Or any of Crystal's other relatives?" She shook her head and I took a deep breath. "Right. Well…" I wasn't looking forward to having to talk to someone about the death of their only sister, but it had to be done. I manned up and asked Max for Christine's phone number, and then said, "Could you give her a call tonight, please? Let her know that I'll be calling tomorrow."

"Sure thing."

I couldn't think of anything more to ask, so I gave Max my card and told him to get in touch with me if he thought of anything else.

As Samantha and I headed out and down to the parking lot, I asked her what she thought of Max.

"He seems sweet," she said. "Pretty upset."

"Seems like he really loved her."

"Yeah." She nodded. "It's every stripper's dream – marry a rich guy and settle down. But not Crystal's dream. And he's not even that rich."

"But he treated her well."

"And she never had anything bad to say about him. Loved him, I guess."

But not enough to tell him that she was a stripper.

———

I GAVE EMILY a quick call, and headed back to the station. As per my luck, the first person I saw when I stepped inside the building was Elwood. He must've just been returning from a cigarette break, because he stank like a chimney. A fat, grumpy chimney.

"Hey!" he said, frowning at me. "What're you doing here again?"

"I'm an investigator, remember? I needed to look at some papers."

He stared at me blankly, like he was processing something hugely complicated. "I thought you were a dealer. I remember you saying that, 'cause my wife's a dealer, too."

"I thought she was your ex."

"Whatever." He waved the inaccuracy away with one hand. "I've never heard of a PI named Tiffany Black."

"Really? Because I helped solve the Ethan Becker murder. Put my life at risk and all that. I was in the papers." Well, ok, just the local paper, but still.

Elwood frowned at me, and I knew he had no clue what I was talking about. But I used this opportunity to slip away and find Emily.

It was good to see Emily again, even though she was busy with work and I didn't want to waste her time. We spent a few seconds complaining about our lives to each other, and then I said, "What's wrong with Elwood?"

Emily laughed. "He's really not that bad. Better than some of the pigs here."

I had to agree. LVMPD officers tend to be overworked and underpaid, and most of them are wonderful people. But some of them – like cops everywhere – really are just pigs. Corrupt, greedy and high on power.

"Did you ever meet the former Mrs. Elwood?"

Emily nodded and I followed her as she walked down the hall. "Yeah, at the LEO's ball last year. Gorgeous woman – all Amazonian curves and beautiful blonde waves."

"Huh. Elwood said I looked like her."

Emily made a face. "Elwood thinks every woman looks like her, now that she's left him. Wait here."

I stood outside the Records Room and waited for a few minutes, taking in the noise and bustle of the station. The place was well-ventilated and studiously bland, but I could still catch a whiff of gun oil, a hint of cigarette smoke and sweat.

Two young officers were standing in a corner, laughing about something, and a group of five older men stood around a desk arguing.

I was trying to guess what they were arguing about – interrogation tactics? Who their lead suspect was? The Bears game? – when Emily walked out of the room with a file in her hand.

She passed it over to me and said, "It's the file you asked for. Crystal Macombe's case was only closed a few days ago, so you can sit over there and go through the file, but you can't copy anything or take notes."

30

I thanked her and headed toward the tiny conference room she'd pointed out. I wasn't sure what I was looking for, but I thumbed through all the pages of the file anyway, desperately hoping something would jump out at me.

There were photos of Crystal's lifeless body, gory and tough to look at. There was the autopsy report, which I deciphered as concluding that she was "stabbed to death, probably by one person." And there were the obligatory interviews – with her boyfriend, Max; with her flatmate, Samantha; with the director of the Casino Kings, Sam Rampell; with people living in houses on the street where she was killed. But the neighbors had heard nothing that night, and neither Max nor Sam said anything interesting or revealing.

I went over the file once more, frowning and biting my lip as I tried to find something I'd missed, but there was nothing. Nada. Whoever was behind Crystal's death, I wouldn't find him by reading this report.

I closed the file with a sigh and left reluctantly when the clock hands had moved too far. I'd be late for my shift, so I said a hurried goodbye to Emily, and sped home to change.

The moment I opened my front door, I noticed the envelope lying on the floor. I thought it was just junk mail, so I locked the door behind me and picked it up.

There was a sheet of letter size paper folded inside the envelope, and I unfolded it to read the single line of printed text.

It said, "You ruin my life, I'll ruin yours."

I looked up and glanced around quickly, as though whoever wrote it might be lurking, watching me.

My condo is small and sparsely furnished. The front door opens into a tiny sitting area, with an open-space kitchen and dining area behind it. There was nobody in this room, so I crept to the bedroom door and glanced inside. It was empty.

I couldn't hear any sounds either – no sounds of somebody breathing, or trying not to make any noise. I checked under the bed, inside the closet, and inside the bathroom. I opened up the curtains and glanced at the tiny verandah that was accessed through the window. Nothing.

My breath came out in a rush, and I realized my ears were pounding with the sound of my blood. I took a moment to sit down on the edge of the bed, and tried to get my heart rate down to normal.

Who could've sent this letter? My brain raced around, trying to think of people who hated me, but I couldn't come up with much. Green Eyes might hate me if he thought I was trying to cause trouble for him, but he had no way of knowing that I'd talked to the cops. He didn't even know who I was or where I lived, which was really quite a shame.

If Crystal had really been murdered, her killer might hate me, but I'd barely even talked to anyone yet. When I'd worked for my previous client, Sophia, I'd uncovered a casino fraud ring at The Riverbelle Casino—a group of twelve casino employees whose members included Mr. Beard and Beady Eyes, the two thugs who'd backroomed me earlier. All the guys involved probably hated me, but they were all behind bars now. In short, there was no reason for anyone to send me a strange, one-line hate letter.

I glanced at it again. It must be a joke. Or maybe it was meant for somebody else and got slipped under my door by mistake.

Yeah, that made sense. It was probably meant for old Mrs. Weebly, who lived two doors down. She was eighty-four years old, an overly-active member of the Home Owners' Association, and constantly poking her nose in other people's business, so the "you ruined my life" line made sense. She'd probably tattled about someone's extra-marital affair, or given someone advice they didn't want to hear. She was always giving people stupid advice – just last week, she'd told me that any job which required a woman to stay out till four in the morning was probably the Devil's work.

"In my day," she'd continued, "a woman like you would stay home and look pretty. A woman needs a man she can rely on, a man she can lean on. Of course, you'll never find a man like that if you keep working all through the night."

And then she'd given me a stern, disapproving look and walked away.

I glanced at the clock and snapped back to reality. I had more urgent problems than this stupid letter – if I didn't rush, I'd be late for work and be docked an hour's pay. So I pushed the letter to the back of my mind, slid into my stupid red and black dealer's outfit and raced out the door.

I speed-walked the couple of blocks up to The Treasury Casino, ignoring the bustle of tourists and the noise of their excitement. I was focusing on not being late for work, and whenever I remembered the letter, I reminded myself that it had actually been meant for Mrs. Weebly. Before I knew it, I was standing in the casino pit, taking up my position behind a blackjack table, and allowing myself to sink into the world of twenty-four hour gambling.

I've worked as a dealer for many years now, and the sights and sounds of the pit feel like my personal security blanket: the jingle of the slot machines, the loud chatter and laughter. The bright lights and gaudy carpets, the wild-eyed gamblers and the exhausted cocktail waitresses.

The job isn't as glamorous as many non-locals think, but it's not as bad as many other jobs out there. Sure, this job's taught me to deal with belligerent drunks, overly-handsy young men and gamblers who've lost their rent money and want to take it out on the dealer – but it pays my bills, and I'm thankful for that.

At least until I have my PI gig sorted out and I can waltz out of this overly bright gambling-addict's paradise.

As I smiled my fake, happy smile, dealt cards and chatted with the gamblers, only a tiny part of my brain was focusing on work. Another tiny part – the part that I couldn't control with my near non-existent willpower – was scanning the crowd in the hopes of seeing Green Eyes. If he were a tourist, he'd visit some casino floors, and though I wasn't sure how I'd recognize him without his ski-mask, I couldn't help but indulge in a bit of wishful thinking.

The rest of my brain was busy remembering the contents of Crystal Macombe's police report – was there anything in it I was overlooking?

I mentally replayed the conversation I'd had with Max. There was no big arrow pointing toward anyone in particular, but I worried about Crystal's secret life as a stripper. That was something the police hadn't known about or looked into, and I wondered if Crystal had seen or heard something at the strip club which might have led to someone wanting to get rid of her. And then there were the photos, and her "stalker friend."

Something about the stalker's photos was bothering me, and I was determined to find out what it was.

SEVEN

My fantasies didn't become reality during my shift – no matter how often I looked around, I didn't spot Green Eyes on the casino floor. I took the same route home, but he didn't fall from the sky again. I hit the sack disappointed, sure that he'd left Vegas and that I'd never see him again.

I woke up the next morning to sound of my cell phone buzzing, once again. The number wasn't one I knew, so I let it ring out. But then it rang again, and I groaned. The noise was bugging me, and I answered grumpily, expecting it to be someone enquiring about my long-distance calling plan.

Instead, it was a woman claiming her name was Stacey Rosenberg and that she worked for All American Insurance.

Immediately, I said, "I'm not interested."

There was silence for a second and then she said in a chilly voice, "I'm the Assistant Claims Investigation Manager."

I yawned and rubbed my eyes. "Are they making managers cold call? Or do they just call everyone a manager, now?"

I heard a deep sigh, and then she spoke slowly, like she was talking to a toddler who only understood very basic words. "We are investigating the theft of the Van Gogh."

I had no idea what she meant, so I said, "That's nice." It was far too early in the morning for me to have a conversation of this length. I needed coffee and breakfast, maybe a slice of cake, before I could talk.

"I spoke to Detective Elwood and he said you may have seen something."

I heard the words "Detective Elwood" and tried to focus. This might not be a telemarketer. "I'm sorry. Who is this?"

I heard another deep sigh. "Somehow, I'd thought you'd be smarter."

My narrowed my eyes. "I am smart! But you just woke me up after four hours of sleep and I haven't had my coffee yet. So you'll excuse me if I'm more interested in figuring out what's for breakfast than your silly Van Gogh."

The woman sighed again. She was really big on sighing. "I'll call again in a few hours," she said, and hung up.

I looked at my phone in annoyance. Twice in a row I'd been woken by a phone call; I was too grumpy and sleepy to care much about whatever she'd been saying, but after I got a large mug of instant coffee and a chocolate-chip muffin inside me, realization dawned.

Before I could hurt myself by hitting my head against the wooden dining table, I pulled out my phone and gave Stacey Whatshername a call.

"Sorry about earlier," I said. "I've had my coffee now and the world's making sense again. What were you saying about a stolen Van Gogh?"

I heard yet another sigh from the other end of the line, and what sounded like a young girl's voice saying, "Brrrrrrr-eeee!"

I quickly added, "This isn't a bad time, is it?"

"Not worse than any other. As I tried to say earlier, I'm investigating the theft of a Van Gogh from Ascend Towers, and Detective Elwood says you may have witnessed it. Can I ask you a few questions?"

"Sure. Would you like me to come in to your office to talk to you?" It wasn't just guilt or helpfulness that prompted my question – I was hoping Stacey would tell me something about what had happened. I was still trying to convince myself that Green Eyes couldn't be a burglar, and maybe Stacey knew something about it. Maybe she even knew who he was, and where he was staying.

"Actually, that'd be great," she said. "When's good for you?"

"The sooner the better. I can be there in about forty-five minutes."

Stacey gave me the address for AAI, and I hung up, hoping I'd be able to learn something interesting about Green Eyes.

———

I STOPPED BY Glen's apartment on my way out. He's a friend I made recently – he lives downstairs in my building, and is a retired baker who constantly makes far too many cupcakes and pastries. Which is wonderful, because I get to take the extras home. He's also handsome and intelligent, and I've always thought that he'd be the perfect boyfriend for Nanna.

He was having coffee, and invited me in for a cup, but I shook my head. "I'm just stepping out to meet someone. Thought I'd say hi."

"Well, stop by again later. I might have something for you to take home."

He gave me a big wink, and I smiled. "Can I pick up anything for you on my way home? Do you need baking stuff? Flour? Sugar?" I frowned and tried to think of other supplies, but I was clueless.

"You could get me some heart-shaped sprinkles," Glen said. "They should keep them in the baking section."

I nodded. "Sure thing. And you haven't seen anyone suspicious hanging out nearby, have you?"

Glen shook his head. Our building doesn't have any security – other than an empty lobby and a couple of fake security cameras. "Why?" he said. "Should I be concerned?"

"Oh, no. I found a note under my door the other day, but it must've been meant for Mrs. Weebly."

Glen smiled. "A lot of people probably want to send her notes."

I nodded and was about to leave when he said, "Maybe when you stop by again, my new girlfriend will be here."

I started to frown and stopped myself just in time. "New girlfriend?"

"Yes." Glenn peered at me nervously. "She's a bit – you might not – not everyone thinks we should be together. But I hope you'll like her."

I smiled at him reassuringly. It sounded like he was dating someone much younger than himself, and while I hadn't expected him to turn around and date someone in her twenties, I wasn't going to judge him if he was. As long as he broke up soon, and started dating someone more suitable. Like Nanna.

"I'm sure I'll like her," I told him, and I promised myself that even if I didn't, I'd be polite to her, for Glenn's sake.

THE AAI OFFICE was in a tall, mirrored building near the Vegas Convention Centre. There was a parking lot opposite, and a low, two-storey office building with a sign advertising skydiving lessons. A large board in front of the mirrored building informed me that office space was available for lease, but I ignored it and made my way up to the AAI floor, where a receptionist directed me to Stacey's office.

I crossed an open-space area, full of unhappy-looking employees typing away on their PCs, and knocked on Stacey's open door. I was sure the cubicled workers envied Stacey her tiny office, but to me, it all seemed pretty bland for a workspace, especially compared to the crazy place I called work.

The carpets in the AAI office were light grey instead of brightly pattered, the lights seemed dimmer than the casino lights, and there were obviously no scantily-clad cocktail waitresses hovering around. The only noise in here was that of the hard workers tippy-tapping away at their keyboards, and the occasional murmur of some official-sounding conversation. The walls were blank and beige, and Stacey's desk was organized neatly, with stacked files on one side, and a couple of photo frames facing away from me.

Stacey was a slightly chubby woman in her mid-forties, with dark hair pulled back severely, and a facial expression that said, "I'm just about to throw up my hands and give up."

She ushered me in politely, and spoke slowly and calmly, like a woman trying to bury her stress deep, deep down. We jumped straight into business, and she explained to me that AAI had insured the Van Gogh that had been stolen from Ascend Towers. They were working with Detective Elwood, but they also had their own private investigator looking into the case.

"Right," I said. "Are you the investigator working the case?"

She shook her head, no, and was about to say something when the cause of her stress ran into the room, holding her arms apart like wings, her vocal cords making a noise that alternated between a hum and a screech. She came to an abrupt stop beside me, and stared at me curiously. "Who are you?"

"I'm Tiffany Black," I said. "Who are you?"

She looked about eight, and had curly brown hair. "I'm a plane," she replied, "I'm a delayed flight."

She made a high-pitched screeching noise and ran out of the room.

Stacey sighed and blinked slowly. "That's Sarah."

"Your daughter?"

She nodded. "She had a fever this morning and I couldn't find a sitter, so I brought her in with me. Like I need more reasons to make my life miserable."

I knew people liked to hear nice things about their kids, so I racked my brains to come up with something. "She seems uh, very creative."

Stacey rolled her eyes. "Too creative. What were we talking about?"

"Are you a PI?"

"No, I just manage our team. And now Jenny, the PI looking into this, has taken off."

I frowned and sat up straighter. "How do you mean?"

"She called in last night and said she's taking off for a few months. Unpaid leave – it's a family emergency. Said she'd mail in her leave application and she's heading out of town."

We stared at each other, both thinking the same thing. Who does that kind of thing in this economy?

Sarah ran into the room again before either of us could say anything.

"Have you been to Europe?" she asked me.

I shook my head, no. "Have you?"

"Yep. I'm flying to Paris now, and then I'm flying to Amsterdam and then I'm coming back to refuel. I'm a busy plane 'cause I'm so popular."

I smiled politely. "That's nice."

Stacey said, "Sarah, don't you think you should sit down now and do some quiet drawing?"

Sarah shook her head. "I can't be late, takeoff is, 3, 2, 1…" and she ran away, flapping her arms and making a screeching noise.

Stacey sighed. "I wish I could get her to listen to me."

I had nothing to say to that. I knew that kids were crazy, and their moms were even crazier for having them. So I said, "Did you want me to tell you what I saw that morning?"

"Yes, let's get this done."

I repeated the story of Green Eyes' jump once again. She took a few notes, and asked me a few questions – what was he wearing, was there anyone else nearby, and what was his car like?

As I cast my mind back to the visual image of Green Eyes driving away, I remembered his number plate. The first three numbers jumped out at me, and I repeated them back to Stacey.

She nodded. "I'll call my contact at the DMV and ask them to run a trace. Do you remember anything else?"

I shook my head. "No. But who's going to work on your investigation now?"

Sarah ran into the room once more, making a buzzing noise, but she caught the expression on her mother's face and ran out immediately.

"I'm not sure," Stacey told me. "Our claim adjusters are busy with other cases for now, and Jenny was the only PI on our payroll. And now my boss is really angry at me because Jenny quit. Like that's my fault."

"I'm an accredited PI," I said hopefully. "I can help out if you'd like."

Stacey looked at me carefully. "Thanks. But I can't really hire you to investigate this because you're a witness."

It was my turn to sigh. It had been worth a shot.

"Besides," Stacey said, "You're sure you saw all this, right?"

I frowned. "Of course."

"It's just that…"

"What?"

"Jenny said she talked to a witness in the building next door who has insomnia, and that guy saw nothing."

I stared at Stacey. "When did Jenny tell you this?"

"Just before she said she was taking off for a few months."

I tried to think logically. "Maybe the guy she talked to has bad eyesight. Or maybe he fell asleep without knowing it."

We were silent for a few seconds, both lost in our own thoughts, and then Stacey said, "I think you can do something else for me."

"Oh?"

"There's a cocktail party tomorrow night honoring our former mayor. And all the local big-shots will be there, including Jeremy. The other investigators are busy and can't make it, but you should go. You could talk to Jeremy, since he doesn't know who you are. I've got an invite here. We'll pay you, of course."

I smiled at that last line. Money was always good. "Who's Jeremy?"

"Oh right. You don't know. He's the guy whose painting was stolen."

I tried not to look too thrilled. "So you want me to talk to him?"

"That's the idea. Just ask him what's going on, if he's got any suspects in mind, that kind of stuff. It's five hundred for the job, plus free drinks at the party." Stacey pulled open a desk drawer and I watched her rummage around before she emerged with a square envelope in her hand. "Here," she said, handing it over to me.

I pulled out the sleek, heavy invite.

"Dear Mr. and Mrs. Smith," it began, "You are cordially invited to…"

"I'm Mrs. Smith?" I said, and Stacey smiled.

"They won't check your ID. You just need to show this invite to get in, and then you can go have fun. You could take a date, too."

I nodded, making a mental note that I'd have to take tomorrow night off from work at the casino. "Ok. I'll do my best with Jeremy."

Stacey looked relieved. "Thanks. Hang on a second, and I'll get a copy of the subcontractor contract."

I spent a few minutes filling out the paperwork and then Stacey handed me a file to go through. It had a couple of photos of Jeremy – one of them was his official passport photo, and the rest looked like they'd been snapped through a telephoto lens. I read the brief story of his life that accompanied the photos – Vegas businessman, pretty successful, married with two kids, yadayada – and then we said our goodbyes. As I walked toward the exit, I noticed Sarah racing through the office making a high-pitched screeching noise. She ran up to me, sputtered to a stop, and said, "I'm going to stop over in London, now."

"That's nice," I told her, and watched her start up slowly before she ran away again.

As I headed back toward my car, I smiled to myself and thought about what I'd say to Jeremy at the party tomorrow. I was hoping it would go well and that he'd tell me something interesting about the theft. Of course, there was something I needed to check up on first.

EIGHT

I stepped into my car and made a phone call. After I was transferred through, the phone rang five times before Elwood answered with a grunt.

"This is Tiffany Black," I said, trying to sound friendly and professional. Instead, I came off sounding like a cheery airhead.

"What is it?"

I'm all for honesty, but a fake-friendly act on Elwood's part might've been nice. "Have you, um, heard anything else about the theft?"

"Police business. Can't talk about it."

"Well, um, did you hear anything about an insomniac who was up and watching all night?"

I could feel Elwood frowning. "Have you been talking to the woman at AAI? Sharon?"

"Stacey. And yes, I have. Did she tell you…?"

"We've cased the area for witnesses."

"And found…?"

Elwood snorted derisively. Of course. He wasn't about to tell me what he'd learnt, but it had been worth a try. And his annoyance made me think that he'd found nothing. Even though what I was sensing might have been just his regular, everyday, having-to-talk-to-people kind of annoyance.

I tried a different tack. "Did you talk to Jenny, the investigator from AAI?"

Elwood made another guttural sound to indicate more annoyance. "Damn PIs. Don't know why they bother."

"Umm, so...did you talk to her?"

"Did you?"

Ha! I assumed Elwood's question meant that he hadn't. "She's not answering her phone and she's not in Vegas."

"Hmm."

That summed up how I felt about Jenny, too. A mysterious witness who claimed nothing happened, and then a mysterious "family emergency" that had Jenny taking off for a few months.

Elwood said, "How do you know about Jenny?"

"Stacey. The manager at AAI."

"Have you talked to Jenny?"

"No."

"And you stand by your story?"

I shrugged, even though he couldn't see me. "I don't know why I wouldn't."

"Ok, then. Anything else you want to tell me?"

I sighed. I didn't know anything else about the theft. "No."

"Bye."

He hung up and I stared down at my phone for a moment. I wondered if Elwood even had any friends – he was always such a strange kind of grumpy.

I pulled out of the AAI parking lot and stopped by Albertson's for groceries. I strolled through the shiny, florescent-lit aisles, looking for the sprinkles Glenn had mentioned, and remembered that I needed more instant coffee, and maybe some snacks and chocolate bars. And maybe something to eat for lunch.

It was late afternoon by the time I got back to my condo, and when I walked out the elevator and got to my door, I stood still for a second, remembering the envelope I'd found yesterday. I glanced both ways down the dimly-lit corridor, wondering if someone was watching me. But it was quiet, and empty of lurkers.

I turned my key in the lock, and pushed the door open to find another white envelope lying in the middle of the floor.

I took a deep breath and tried to ignore the pounding in my ears. It was just an envelope.

I dropped my bag of groceries near the front door, stepped inside and looked around carefully. I couldn't see anybody else in the living area, kitchen or dining room. I took a deep breath, and checked through my bedroom, closet and bathroom. Nobody.

I exhaled, locked my front door and went and sat on my couch.

The envelope stared up at me from the floor.

I wanted to curl up into a little ball and pretend that none of this existed. "It's probably meant for Mrs. Weebly," I told myself. "They got the wrong door again."

But I wasn't convinced. The envelope looked thicker this time, somehow more ominous.

I'd never know if I didn't look. I took a deep breath, picked the envelope off the floor and peeked under the flap. Inside were a bunch of glossy photographs.

My mind went numb; my hands took control and pulled out the photos. There were about thirty, all taken today, all of me.

There I was, parking at the AAI office, and there I was, walking up to the building. Me coming out of the building. Another of me getting into my car, sitting in the car and talking on my phone. Me getting out at the store parking lot; me again, walking into Albertsons.

I felt dizzy and weak. I shoved them back into the envelope, and leaned against the sofa. What was going on?

I closed my eyes and images of the photos drifted before me. I saw the half-empty parking lots, lined with palm trees and devoid of any other people. I felt sick, as though I'd run a marathon and was ready to throw up.

I opened my eyes again and stared at the benign white envelope, puffy with its pregnant contents. I remembered Crystal, and the photos she'd received of herself. How could she have laughed them off as a joke?

My tiny condo felt big and empty. I couldn't deal with this alone. Before I knew what I was doing, I'd walked over to my bag, pulled out my phone, and dialed a number.

Stone picked up after one ring. "Hey."

"Are you busy? Can you come over for a minute?"

There was a split-second pause and then he said, "Are you ok?"

"Of course I'm ok!" I hadn't quite processed the photos, but my fear exploded into a mass of irritation and bravado. "Why wouldn't I be? I can take care of myself."

"Hmm," he said. I thought I heard a smile in his voice, and I felt a bit better. Even though I wasn't sure what was going on, I knew I'd done the right thing by calling Stone.

"I'll be there in a few minutes," Stone said and hung up.

I put away my groceries, doing my best to stay calm and to think about anything other than the photos.

Five minutes later, there was a knock on the door, and I opened it quickly, my heart singing with relief. "Stone!"

I smiled and almost hugged him. I stopped myself just in time – Stone isn't the hugging type. He's a quiet, serious, ex-Special Forces guy with angular, chiseled jawbones and deep, dark eyes. Today, like every time I've seen him, he was wearing dark blue jeans, a white shirt and formal black shoes. The shirt hinted at some serious muscle underneath, and the shoes sparkled like they belonged to someone with an unhealthy need for cleanliness and order. Which he had, considering some of the comments he'd made in the past about the state of my apartment.

He stepped inside and looked around my condo. "What's wrong?"

"What makes you think anything's wrong?" I smiled, trying to act normal, and headed over to the kitchen. "Would you like some coffee? Chocolate?"

I handed him one of the chocolate bars I'd picked up at Albertson's, and Stone studied the packaging. "Filled with delicious strawberry cream," he read out drily. He glanced up at the jar of instant coffee I'd placed on the counter top, and then he looked at me. I thought I saw a flicker of amusement in his dark eyes. "Why the sudden generosity?"

I shrugged. "No reason."

Stone put the chocolate back on the countertop and said, "Thanks, but no thanks."

I'd figured as much. Stone didn't seem to have an ounce of fat on him, and he probably looked that way by never eating cream-filled chocolates.

"What's wrong?" he asked again. "You sounded kind of freaked on the phone."

"Oh, yeah." My heart sank. I didn't want to face the facts again, but I had to, so I nodded at the envelope lying on my coffee table. "I got some mail."

Stone raised one eyebrow at me, and picked up the envelope. He opened it without asking permission, pulled out the photos and flipped through them. When he looked at me again, the angles of his face seemed to have hardened. "What's going on?"

I shook my head, and sat down at the edge of the sofa. "No idea."

Stone looked at a particular photo again. "Taken today?"

"Yep."

"Any other photos?"

"No, but…" I took a deep breath and went to find my junk mail pile. Yesterday's envelope was there, and I handed it over to Stone, who pulled out the one-line letter, read it, and put it back.

He looked at me questioningly, and I shrugged. "I thought it might've been meant for Mrs. Weebly."

Stone's eyebrows moved together a fraction of an inch. "Mrs. Weebly?"

"You know, old Mrs. Weebly."

Stone shook his head.

"We ran into her one day," I said. "She told you that you should get married? That the Devil lives in bachelors? That unmarried young men like you are more likely to be criminals?"

"Oh, *that* Mrs. Weebly."

The corners of Stone's mouth curved up slightly. Stone hardly every smiles, and I've never heard him laugh.

"In that case," he said, "I can understand someone sending her this letter. But it's not meant for her."

"No."

We looked at each other seriously.

"And you're not even working on any new cases," Stone said.

"Actually…"

His left eyebrow went up a notch. "Really? I just talked to you last week."

"What can I say?" I shrugged with mock-modesty. "It never rains, but it pours."

"Sure." He looked at me skeptically, so I filled him in on my work, not bothering to mention how charming Green Eyes had seemed.

"Hunh," he said after listening to me. "So we've got some suspects now. This Green Eyes guy and whoever killed Crystal."

"You think she was murdered?"

"Definitely."

I looked at the envelope again and sighed. The intense fear I'd felt was now being replaced with something similar to resignation. "Now what?"

"You gotta be careful. Carla tells me you haven't been going to KravMaga classes."

"Hey, I wasn't working on anything, and besides, Carla's scary."

"She's a KravMaga instructor. I'd be worried if she wasn't scary." Stone looked at me seriously. "At least you've been doing shooting practice with me."

"Only because you've been dragging me out once a week."

"And aren't you thankful now?"

I rolled my eyes and looked at him. Our eyes stayed locked for a few seconds: his, amused and confident; mine, increasingly unsure. Stone and I are friends, but sometimes, when our eyes stay locked like that, I got a funny feeling deep down, and I wondered if maybe we're more than friends. But he's never said anything – and neither have I. We're just friends. For now.

I was the first to look away, as usual. I had a brief, fleeting fear that my hair was a mess, and I reached up to smooth it down.

"We don't know what this guy wants," Stone said. "We don't even know who the guy is. We'll drop off the photos and the letter with the cops and have them dust for prints."

"That's a good idea." I looked at Stone, surprised that I hadn't thought of it myself. Some investigator I was. But then again, I'd been too scared to think properly.

I called Emily to see if she was at work, and we took Stone's car down to the police station. Thankfully, we didn't see Elwood this time – we spent a few minutes chatting with Emily, explaining what was going on, and then we left.

I was just stepping into his car when my stomach grumbled loudly.

Stone looked at me. "No lunch?" I shook my head, no, and he said, "On a diet?"

I frowned at him. "Why would I be on a diet?"

"No reason." Stone began driving. "Want to get something to eat?"

I stopped frowning and breathed in deeply. Stone was staring straight ahead, watching the road with studied seriousness. "Yeah," I said, "How about a burger?"

We saw golden arches ahead, and Stone turned into the parking lot. I went in and ordered a Big Mac with fries and a Coke. Stone ordered nothing.

When my order was ready, I grabbed my tray and we headed over to a booth in the corner. Stone watched me as I dug into my fries.

"Not hungry?" I asked.

"Not interested in getting a heart attack."

I ignored him and bit into my burger. Glorious meat, cheese and mayo. Who in their right mind would want to give up all this?

My phone rang and I gulped down an overly large mouthful of food.

"Hi, Samantha." I sounded cheerier than I felt.

"Hi, Tiffany. How's the investigation going?"

I stifled a groan and watched Stone text someone. In between the AAI meeting with Stacey and the scary photos, I hadn't gotten a chance to really look into Crystal's murder.

"It's ok," I fibbed. Well, it wasn't a complete lie – it was ok if I had some hope the investigation would get somewhere. "I'm heading off to my shift in a bit, so I'll give you a call tomorrow."

"About anything particular?"

"Just whether you know anything more about Crystal's stalker. And I'd like to talk to some of her friends on the movie."

"Casino Kings."

"Yeah. Where's it being shot?"

"Tremonte. Part of the pit's portioned off."

"Ok, well –"

"I can tell you about the stalker now. Crystal never mentioned it to me."

"Oh."

Samantha heard the disappointment in my voice and said, "But I'll text you her friend Minnie's number."

"Ok, thanks."

Well, at least it was a start. We hung up, and Stone said, "I assume that was Crystal's friend?"

I nodded, and gobbled up another French fry.

"You shouldn't fib," he said.

I shrugged. "Wasn't really a fib. Don't you ever?"

The corners of his mouth twitched in amusement, but he didn't answer.

That reminded me. "Speaking of fibs, would you like to go to a party tomorrow night, honoring Oscar Goodman? I've got an invite, and I could do with a plus one."

Stone raised one eyebrow. "Party with all the Vegas hot-shots? How'd you get an invite?"

I smiled and did a modest hand-flipping thing. "I have my ways." Stone didn't look convinced, so I added, "We'll be going as Mr. and Mrs. Smith."

His eyes twinkled and he said, "Sure. We can be Mr. and Mrs. Smith."

I almost choked on my burger. Was there a sexy subtext beneath his words, or was that just me? "So you'll go with me?"

He shrugged. "Why not? It's a glorified networking event, I might as well try to drum up some business."

I looked at him skeptically. Stone seemed to be doing pretty well for himself, and I wasn't sure that his business needed much more drumming up.

Before I could say anything, Stone asked, "When's your shift?"

"In an hour or so. I guess we should head back to my condo."

He nodded and said, "I'll walk you to The Treasury."

"You don't have to."

"And I'll walk you back home when your shift ends."

"It ends at three a.m."

"Ok."

I looked at him warily. "Are you going to escort me around everywhere?"

He leaned back in his seat and looked at me. "That's the plan."

The last time Stone had escorted me around, my money-bags client Sophia had been paying his fees. This time, I couldn't afford his services, so I said, "I can't pay you. I'm not exactly rolling in the dough, remember?"

"That's ok. You get the special 'Friends In Trouble Discount.'"

"I still can't afford this."

"We'll work something out."

I shook my head, no. "I can take care of myself."

Stone didn't say anything, so I finished my meal and we headed out.

———

A FEW MINUTES later, I'd changed into my uniform, and Stone was walking me to The Treasury.

I'd tried to explain that I didn't need his presence and that I'd be fine, but Stone just shook his head. Finally, he said, "I won't always be here. If something comes up, I'll need to get to work. You can take care of yourself then. But make sure you go to KravMaga class this week."

I was on an early shift tonight, and once it started, I entered my zombie-like dealer state. I clapped my hands out behind the blackjack table, dealt cards, and made some kind of joke. At the same time, I allowed myself to wonder just what was going on. Was somebody watching me right now, maybe taking photos of me? Maybe this was what it felt like to be famous – it was as though I were a celebrity, but without the perks.

Thousands of security cameras were scattered throughout the casino floor, and when I glanced up, I could see multitudes of them on the ceiling, their red lights blinking away. If anyone came here to photograph me, I could ask security to pull up tonight's video footage, and then I'd know who was stalking me.

The thought should've made me feel better, but it didn't.

NINE

By the time my shift finished, a drunk guy had spilled his pink cocktail all over my uniform. He was a little embarrassed about it, but the pink hardly showed up against the red and black, so it hadn't been the worst of nights. Plus I'd remembered to tell my manager that I was taking the night off the following evening.

I changed out of my uniform and stepped out into the warm, autumn night. As soon as I took a few steps forward, Stone materialized at my side, and I almost jumped in surprise.

"Where were you?" I asked, but he just smiled.

The thought that I hadn't noticed Stone was disturbing. If I hadn't seen Stone, I wouldn't see whoever was stalking me. It was all the tourists – they formed a kind of moving, squawking, human foliage, so that even with all those bright neon lights, a guy could hide just about anywhere.

"I'm not going home," I said, even though he'd probably noticed already. "Nanna sent me a text and asked me to go and watch her play poker at The Tremonte." Stone nodded, and kept on walking beside me. Maybe he hadn't gotten the message yet, so I said, "You really don't have to come with me. I'll be fine."

"It'll be fun watching Nanna play," Stone said, and I rolled my eyes. He was lying; it'd be like watching grass grow. I was only going because of Nanna's constant bugging.

The Tremonte's low and medium-stakes poker tables were off toward the back of the gaming area. As I headed that way, I noticed that a large area behind the table games section was partitioned off, and assumed that's where they were shooting Casino Kings.

Nanna was settled at a table with seven other players, and she waved when she saw me walk in. I waved back and looked around – there was a bar located conveniently nearby, so I grabbed a stool, ordered a club soda, and settled in to watch. Stone sat next to me and ordered a black coffee.

"Long night ahead?" I asked, and immediately regretted the question.

Stone shrugged. "You never know."

I assumed he was working some job, and I didn't want to ask for details. He pulled out his smartphone and began typing away.

"Emails?" I asked.

Stone made a facial shrug. "Some. Plus a bunch of surveillance reports I need to check and some other random stuff."

The noise of the casino pit was a bit muted in this section. The jingle of slots and occasional whoops, groans and laughter drifted in, but mostly we could hear the chatter at the tables: players calling, raising and folding. I kept an eye on Nanna's table, but she'd folded and I wasn't really interested in the other players.

"This game sucks," I heard someone at Nanna's table say, and Stone and I exchanged a glance.

More voices drifted over to us. The dealer at Nanna's table was saying, "Please don't splash the pot," and Stone and I glanced over to see who the newbie player was.

He wasn't hard to miss — an obese, red-faced man wearing a bright red-and-white checked shirt. Nanna was good at picking out fools at poker tables, and she was also good at getting them to part with their money.

"Hey," the red-faced man said to the dealer, "Give me a break, huh? I'm the one tipping you."

I felt my eyes narrow involuntarily. It wasn't fun dealing with the clueless, drunk player. The other poker players looked stiff-faced, clearly trying to keep their annoyance in check.

Nanna was tight-lipped. She's never good at keeping her thoughts to herself, and I could see her emotions fighting an internal battle, the desire to win some money off the guy against the desire to give him a piece of her mind. I smiled to myself.

"Seems like she picked a good table," I said, more to myself than to Stone.

He grunted something in response, and put his phone away.

A new hand had been dealt, and the play continued smoothly — until Nanna won.

The red-face man was one of the three players still in the game, and when Nanna revealed her hand, he scowled at her and said, "You're cheating."

The whole table went quiet and looked at Nanna. I held my breath and hoped that she'd be polite. She smiled and said, "Honey, nobody needs to cheat to win against you."

The other players laughed, and even the dealer looked suspiciously happy.

"That's it!" The man stood up and faced Nanna. "You better show me what card you've got up your sleeve."

Nanna said, "And you'd better show us the roast chicken you stole from the dinner buffet."

She was sitting demurely, her thin, wrinkled hands folded neatly together, and play had stopped.

The man yelled, "You stupid old bitch! Why don't you just go and die already?"

The table went quiet and everyone stared at the man.

Nanna said, "Why don't you go to a fat farm instead of a Vegas buffet?"

I smiled, proud of her but embarrassed at the same time. Two bouncers were heading their way now, and I hoped Nanna would be able to time her "sweet old lady act" perfectly and look helpless. I realized that half the casino floor was watching them, and then suddenly, I felt a chill creeping up the back of my neck. I was being watched.

There was a stillness in the air, and goosebumps were rising along my arms. I couldn't make out what Nanna was saying anymore – all the noise blended together into one cacophonous buzz. I turned around slowly, trying to act casual, trying to ignore the pounding in my chest, as I covertly scanned the area for someone with a camera.

And that's when I saw him. Green Eyes.

TEN

He smiled when our eyes met and I stood up instinctively. "Be back," I managed to mutter to Stone, as I walked toward Green Eyes on autopilot.

It had to be him. The eyes were the same, and so was the height and build. He was wearing a dark, stylishly-cut business suit and a crisp white shirt. Straight, dark brown hair fell across his forehead, and he leaned against the wall, his eyes twinkling with amusement as he watched me make a beeline toward him.

I didn't know what I would say to him. "Did you steal a painting that day?" Or maybe, "Why are you standing there, watching me?" Or maybe even, "Have you been stalking me and taking my photos?"

I was a few feet away from him when he turned and disappeared into a nearby corridor.

I quickened my pace and found myself in the same corridor. There were three elevators on the right side, moving up and down, and a door marked "Fire Escape" next to the elevator closest to me. On the other side of the wall was a door marked, "Employees Only."

Green Eyes was dressed too stylishly to be a casino employee. He could've taken any of the three elevators, but just in case, I opened the Fire Escape door and looked up and down the flights of stairs.

I couldn't see anyone, and there were no tell-tale sounds either – no footsteps going up or down, no quiet breathing.

I stepped out and let the door close behind me. A trio of girls in sparkly cocktail dresses stepped out of one of the elevators, and I watched them blankly as they entered the gaming pit.

I took a deep breath. It had been Green Eyes, I was sure of it. And his running away from me didn't bode well, either. I wanted to believe that he had nothing to do with any kind of crime, but it was time to stop being so naïve. I looked up, and noticed the camera blinking away on the ceiling. And that's when I knew what to do.

I headed back to the bar to find Stone typing away into his phone. The craziness at the poker table had died down, the red-faced obese man was nowhere to be seen, and Nanna was play-ing her cards serenely.

"I need a favor," I said to Stone as I sat down. "Can you get in touch with the friend of yours who works in Tremonte security?"

He gave me a funny look. "What's going on?"

I told him about Green Eyes, and about my plan. He nod-ded wordlessly and walked off, probably in search of his security buddy.

I watched Nanna's poker table as I waited. Nanna had just folded her cards. She had a martini glass by her hand, and occa-sionally, she'd raise the martini glass to her lips, but I never saw the drink diminish.

There was a gorgeous woman sitting at her table now – all big boobs, wavy hair and serious makeup. Every man at the table was glancing at her occasionally, except for a young, curly-haired man sitting next to Nanna. He was chatting with Nanna in a low voice, saying something I couldn't hear. I frowned – something seemed off.

Curly had been at the table when the red-faced man had been there, and now he was making Nanna laugh. She flipped her hand and smiled at him, and my suspicion was confirmed. Curly looked far too wide-eyed and sweet to be anything but a con-man.

Stone walked back to the bar and I smiled hopefully. "What'd you learn?"

"Nothing."

I blinked stupidly. "Huh?"

"I asked my buddy, Steve, to look up the man in the dark suit standing against the wall, and he had a look."

"So? Where'd he go?"

"Steve said he couldn't tell me anything about the man."

I frowned. "Nothing at all?"

"No. Sorry."

I took a deep breath. "Nothing? At all?" I was unable to believe my luck. "Why not?"

"He didn't say, just that he's not allowed to talk about this guy."

I bit my lip unhappily. "Maybe he's a whale," I mused. "Or maybe…"

I let my voice drift off and looked at Stone for suggestions, but he just shrugged.

I sighed and stared vaguely in the direction where Green Eyes had been. Once again, I'd lost him.

A COUPLE OF hands later, Nanna came over to the bar. She chatted with Stone for a bit, something about the coffee here being terrible, and I asked how play was going.

"Not bad," she said, smiling happily.

I looked at her carefully. "And who's that curly-haired guy you keep talking to?"

"Talking?" Nanna raised her eyebrows. "I thought we were flirting."

I closed my eyes and groaned softly. I could feel Stone smiling beside me.

Nanna said, "You're not jealous of me, are you? You've got a perfectly nice man right next to you."

"Thank you," Stone said.

"I'm not jealous," I said to Nanna. "I'm concerned. What's this guy's name?"

"Nathan Jones."

"Sounds like a made-up name," I said. "What's he want?"

"He doesn't *want* anything. He's new to Las Vegas and he's going to take me out for coffee and a snack after a few more hands."

I rubbed my temples and tried not to scream out loud. "He's out to con you," I said.

Nanna crossed her arms. "He is *not* out to con me. I'm not stupid, you know."

Usually.

Just then, Nathan walked over to us and smiled at Nanna. "Is this your grand-daughter?" he asked her. "You don't look old enough to be a grandmother."

I narrowed my eyes, and next to me, Stone coughed suspiciously. Nanna was wearing a sensible mid-length dress and black orthopedic shoes. She's my Nanna and I love her, but she definitely looks old enough to be a grandmother. She looks old enough to be Nathan's grandmother; maybe even his great-grandmother.

Nanna smiled and said, "Oh, stop."

I looked at Nathan. "What're you doing in Vegas?"

He glanced at me with his long-lashed, big blue eyes and told me a story about dropping out of college to play professional poker.

"Hmm," I said. "Good luck with that."

"Thanks." He sounded sincere, and I tried not to roll my eyes.

"We should go," I told Nanna. "Good luck with the rest of the hands."

ELEVEN

Half-way down the Strip, Stone's phone went off, and he looked at it and growled something indecipherable.

"I have to take off," he said. "It's an emergency. You're going to be ok?"

I smiled and tried to look happier than I felt. "Of course! You go ahead. You didn't need to come with me to The Tremonte, either."

He said goodbye, looking like he didn't believe me, and the truth was that the night was making me nervous. It was still too early for the crowds to go home, but as soon as I took a few steps into the side-street I've always used as a shortcut, I felt the shadows pressing in. There were enough streetlights to make the place seem well-lit, but I looked over my shoulder every five seconds until I got to my condo. Once I was safely inside the lobby, I decided that for the time being, I'd be taking the longer East Flamingo Road walk instead.

There were no new envelopes under my door, and a quick check revealed that, thankfully, there were no strangers lurking inside either. I made myself a cup of decaf, but I was still too jittery from my walk back home to finish it.

I slept fitfully that night. It was hard to believe that I'd run into Green Eyes again, and once again, he'd disappeared into thin air. I was glad there were no more creepy photos of me, but my thoughts kept returning to the way Green Eyes had walked away from me.

I woke up early the next morning, and the condo was still devoid of any new mysterious white envelopes. I had a glimmer of hope that maybe whoever had taken my photographs had mixed me up with someone else, or maybe they'd just gotten tired of stalking me. For whatever reason, maybe I was off the hook.

After breakfast, I gave Stacey a call. "Did you run those license-plate numbers?" I asked.

"Yes, do you have a pen and paper handy? Ok, here we go. There are six red Ferraris in Nevada that have license plates starting with those three numbers. Three belong to luxury car rental services. Two were garaged that day, and one was rented by a guy – Donald Hughes – who drove out to the desert with three of his friends. The friends all say they were riding around in the wee hours of the morning, and GPS navigation on the car matches up. One of the cars belongs to a resident who was in Toronto on holiday. The other two cars belong to Nevada residents, both of whom were at home at that time. We're pretty sure they're not lying, but there's no way to prove one hundred percent that they're not. The first car's registered to a Collette Hill, and the second's registered to a Jack Weber."

"Somebody could've broken into one of the car rental garages and taken a car out for a joyride."

"Not likely. Alarms would go off, and the rental agencies would know. I'm sorry – maybe you got the numbers mixed up?"

I sighed. "Maybe I did. Oh well, it was worth a shot."

Once again, I felt like I'd come close to learning Green Eyes' identity, and once again, he'd slipped away.

My next call was to Crystal's sister, Carol. When she answered her phone, I introduced myself, and she said, "Yes, that boyfriend of hers, Max, said you'd be calling."

There was an awkward silence and then I said, "I'm so sorry for your loss."

She sighed. "It's ok. I asked the cops if I needed to come down to Las Vegas, but they said it's ok. Which was good, because it costs money to get one of those last minute flights out. And now Max wants to have the funeral out in LA – I mean, can you believe it? I'm her flesh and blood, and that guy's just known her – what – two years, maybe three?"

I made a sympathetic noise, and tried to think of what to say next. I needn't have bothered, because she started again, "And now Bob's going to have to take time off work and we're going to have fly down for the funeral – I don't know *how* I'm going to fly with three young kids with me."

"How old are your kids?"

"Nine, four and two. Do you have kids?"

"No."

"Yeah, neither did Crystal. These people without kids just don't realize how hard it is to have them. You've got to rearrange your whole life for them, you can't just up and fly over to a different state. Poor Crystal, may God rest her soul."

"Were you close?" I managed to ask.

"Close?" She made a low, derisive noise. "We were like *this*, growing up. But then she became beautiful and popular and decided Nebraska wasn't good enough for her anymore. She flew over to LA and decided to try to be an actress. An actress!"

She made that strange, derisive noise again. "'Course, some people get all the luck, get to follow their dreams. Crystal was an extra in a few movies." I thought I detected a hint of pride in her voice. "Might even have worked out for her. Sometimes I wonder if I should've left Nebraska too, 'stead of staying on and not having a career and such. But Crystal took a risk and look where it got her."

She went quiet for a few seconds, and I took this opportunity to ask, "Did Crystal have any enemies that you knew of? Anyone who might want to hurt her?"

"Lord, no," she said, and then she went on to tell me how friendly Crystal was and how everyone loved her and how popular she'd been in high school. And then she told me how much her kids loved Aunt Crystal, even though she rarely came to visit, now that she was so busy in Hollywood and too cool for Nebraska. Not that she begrudged Crystal any success of course, it's just that she missed her little sister and now the Lord had seen fit to take her.

She went on and on for some time, and I interjected questions whenever she paused to take a breath. After a while, I'd managed to ask her everything I needed to. But I learnt nothing – Carol had only seen Crystal a handful of times since she'd moved down to LA, and knew basically nothing about Crystal's life. In the end, all I had was a higher phone bill.

After I'd managed to extricate myself from that call, I rang Crystal's friend Minnie. I introduced myself once again and explained that I was looking into Crystal's death.

"Damn right," Minnie said. "It didn't make any sense to me at the time."

I agreed. "Can I come over to talk to you about Crystal?"

"Sure. Come over to the movie set at The Tremonte. I'll have a few minutes free at some point. And you can talk to some of the other girls on the set, too."

I thanked her, hung up and slid into the same black slacks and green top I'd worn the day before. They smelled clean enough to me, but I dabbed some perfume on, just in case. I was about to step out when there was a knock at the door. I opened it to find Stone waiting outside.

He looked at me and raised one eyebrow. "Heading out?"

"Just to The Tremonte. What're you doing here?"

"I was in the neighborhood." He stepped inside and looked around. "Any new envelopes?"

"No – maybe the guy forgot about me."

"I'd like to think that. But he's just stopped following you. He won't follow you into a casino or anywhere with security cams."

I looked at Stone thoughtfully. "You don't think this guy's dangerous, do you? I think it's just someone trying to mess with me."

My mind went back to Green Eyes, and the way he'd looked amused to see me. I really didn't want to believe that he was behind the photos.

"You might be right," Stone said. "Someone really dangerous would send proper threats, not just a day's worth of photos."

We looked at each other silently. Neither of us was convinced that the photos were a joke, but there was nothing to do about it, other than wait for the next message or set of photos.

Stone walked me to my car, and said, "I'll stop by your place at seven, and we can go to the ex-mayor's party together. Do you want one of my guys to stick with you today?"

I shook my head. "I'm just running errands along the Strip. I should be fine."

———

MINNIE WAS A gorgeous blonde who looked like she could've been an actress herself. Her hair was pulled back in a severe ponytail, and she worked quickly with her makeup brushes, applying a full face of makeup to an olive-skinned girl who looked about sixteen.

A couple of meters from where she worked, a scene was being shot, over and over again under bright, harsh lights – two guys stood beside a blackjack table arguing with a woman about something. Every time the action started, the whole set went quiet, and after the director yelled "Cut!" a low buzz of chatter erupted, while the director waved his arms around and tried to explain something. Tourists stood around the roped-off border of the set, gawking at the actors for a few seconds, before getting distracted by something else and moving on.

When Minnie was done with the makeup application, we headed over to a quieter section of the set, away from the action.

"We all loved Crystal," Minnie told me. "Hollywood's a tough place, but Crystal knew how to get along with everyone."

"How'd she get her role in Casino Kings?"

Minnie smiled and told me the same thing Samantha had said – that the actress scheduled to play the part had fallen ill, and Crystal was her replacement. "She got along well with the director," Minnie said. "He thought this'd be a great role for her."

"What about any enemies?" Minnie shook her head no, and I said, "Did she have a stalker or anyone following her around?"

71

Minnie looked puzzled and shook her head again. "But maybe someone else will know something," she said. "The cast members all know each other and they hang out sometimes."

She dragged me around the set, introducing me to the cast and grips whenever they weren't in a scene, and running off occasionally to do makeup touch-ups or applications. I explained to everyone I was introduced to that I was looking into Crystal's death, and asked if they knew if she had any enemies, or had they seen anyone following her around?

Everyone I was introduced to either didn't know Crystal, or they told me that Crystal was a lovely person with no enemies. No, they hadn't noticed anyone following her around.

After about an hour and a half of chatting with people and not finding out anything new, I met Lucy, an actress who played a minor love interest in the movie.

"Yeah, I knew Crystal," she said, after Minnie introduced me and explained what I was doing. "She was cool. We hung out at the Indie Movie Convention together, and I was looking forward to working with her."

"Did Crystal have any enemies? Did you notice anyone following her around or taking her photos?"

Lucy looked at me thoughtfully. "You know, now that you mention it…There was this one guy at the Movie Convention who took a lot of photos of her from a distance. I thought he seemed a bit creepy."

I nodded, excited to have finally found something. "Can you describe the guy to me?"

"Sure. Medium height, dark brown hair, average looking."

"Hmm." That was a big help. "Where was the convention held?"

"The MontePatria Casino."

I nodded. Lucy's description wasn't much to go on, but if I could get in touch with someone in the security team at The MontePatria, video footage might pull up something.

I handed Lucy my card and told her to call me if she thought of anything else.

I'd talked to everyone but the director and the chief cameraman by now, so I waited till they took a break, and then introduced myself.

"I'm Sam Rampell," the director said, "And this is Tony Gruen."

Sam Rampell was tall and muscular, with wavy grey hair cut stylishly. I'd guess he was around fifty, and spent two hours a day in the gym. He had twinkling brown eyes, and I could feel the force of his charisma. In contrast, Tony was tall and skinny, and smiled at me shyly.

"I'd love to stay and chat," Sam went on, "But I've got an appointment in five minutes. Why don't you stop by again later this afternoon? Here's my card. And not everyone's on set right now," he added. "Why don't you get a list of everyone from Tony?"

It was a good idea, and Tony found me a printout with a list of names and contact phone numbers. I chatted with Tony for a bit, said goodbye to Minnie, and headed to the quiet café opposite the gift shop.

It was almost lunch-time, but I wasn't really hungry. I did, however, need a minute to think, so I ordered myself a cappuccino and a chocolate-chip muffin, and ran my eyes over the list of movie employees that Tony had given me.

Most of the people who hadn't been on the set today were either actors who weren't needed in the scenes shot in Vegas, or extras who hadn't been needed today. The movie had two co-producers,

Ben McAllister, and Jack Weber; neither of them had been on the set today. Next to the column for contact phone number, there was also a column for "address in Vegas." Most people were staying at The MontePatria, Tremonte or other hotels nearby, but Jack was a local who lived in a gated community in Henderson.

I finished my muffin and coffee, and gave Stone a call. "I'm trying to get access to someone who works security at MontePatria," I said, and explained the situation. Stone said he was onto it, and hung up.

Most people leave Vegas after a few days. There are so few of us locals that we all know each other – Stone had especially good contacts in security, but if he couldn't find someone, I was sure I could find an old high-school classmate, or son of a family friend, who worked over there and could get me through. If nothing else, Nanna would find the son or daughter of one her Old People's Gang friends and put me in touch with them.

But that wasn't necessary. Stone rang back within a few minutes. "I talked to the head of security at MontePatria," he said. "He's happy to help out. An employee of his, guy named Scott Rodriguez, will meet you at reception."

"Small world," I said. Scott and I had been in high-school together. He'd seemed like a nice kid, but we hadn't been particularly close. Most of us who'd been to school together never managed to leave Vegas; we all seemed to work for the casinos in some capacity or the other.

"How about your stalker?" Stone asked. "Any sign?"

"Nope. I guess you're right about him staying away from casinos. Or maybe he's lost interest."

I hung up and headed toward The MontePatria, walking slowly down the Strip and looking over my shoulder once in a while.

The MontePatria Casino is a large, popular casino located near the south end of the Strip. They do booming business no matter what, have large, gaudy water fountains out front, and a massive team of employees.

Scott was lanky, bespectacled and apparently still constantly acne-prone. He came down to meet me, and handed me a guest pass so I could access the security area.

"Kate told me you're trying to be a PI," he said, mentioning another of our old classmates.

I nodded. "You don't have any jobs for me here, do you?"

"No, we're laying people off."

"Really? I thought The MontePatria's profits were up."

He winced. "Profits are up. They're cutting costs so profits *stay* up."

We were silent after that, and as we rode up in the elevator, I texted him the photos of Crystal that were on my phone.

"This her?" he asked, and I nodded.

I followed Scott into the security room. I'd never been inside before, and I glanced around at the dozens of TV screens, relaying everything that was going on down in the pit. I looked away quickly, feeling like a voyeur.

Scott had his own mini-station, with six 21-inch monitors. He pressed a few buttons on his phone, and Crystal's photo appeared on one of the monitors.

"I'll run a facial recognition scan," he told me. "When was this convention?"

I gave him the dates, and Scott pressed a bunch of keys. A rotating circle appeared on his screen, and then a match quickly flashed up.

We watched as Crystal entered the casino that day and headed straight to the Indie Movie Convention. The first thirty minutes of footage were yawn-inducingly boring. We watched as she flipped her hair, greeted some people she knew and was introduced to new people.

Half an hour in, I noticed her glancing over her shoulder.

"There!" I said. "She's looking in that direction."

Scott pulled up a layout of the cameras in the room on one of his monitors.

"This is the feed we're watching now," he said. "She's looking in this direction, so…"

He switched to a different camera, and I saw him. Average height, dark brown hair, and a big camera.

"That's the guy!" I said. "Can we get a better look at him?"

Scott fiddled around with various camera feeds, and we watched the guy walk around, taking photos once in a while. To an outside observer, he looked like just another photography enthusiast. He was even wearing an "I Love Las Vegas" t-shirt that made him look like a regular tourist.

Other than taking a couple of photos of Crystal, the guy did nothing that seemed suspicious. We watched him for another thirty minutes while he took photos, stood around, and finally left. I kept expecting him to do something crazy – maybe walk up to Crystal and threaten her, or at the very least, steal food off the buffet table. But he seemed normal.

"Go back," I told Scott, "Let's watch him walk in."

Scott looked bored, but he played the feed backwards, at a slightly faster speed so we could get through it quicker. I was grateful for the faster speed, because once again, the guy did nothing particularly suspicious.

Scott looked at me. "Now what?"

I took a deep breath. I was out of ideas, and I couldn't lose this one lead I had.

"Run facial recognition," I suggested. "Maybe he came into the casino some other day."

Scott paused the video and clicked some buttons.

"Bingo!" he said. "One other match. The guy came in two weeks ago."

He pulled up the footage, set it to double speed, and we both watched the guy walk into the casino, head into a conference room, and begin to take photo after photo. I frowned. Some of the shots were candid, but in others, he was asking people to pose for him.

"What's going on?" I asked.

It looked like a pretty boring event, full of middle-aged guys in shorts and t-shirts, men who'd clearly never seen the inside of a gym. Half of them wore glasses, and most of them were engrossed in serious-looking conversations. There were the obligatory Vegas chorus girls walking around, trying to pass out brochures, wearing headdresses bigger than their bikinis.

"That's the Pearson Conference Room," Scott said. "I'll look up what was on that day…International Ruby on Rails Developers Conference."

We shared a glance and Scott shrugged. He pulled up the brochure for the event, and we read through it together: "RailsConf, the largest gathering of Ruby on Rails developers in the world, is coming to Las Vegas! Join us and connect with top Rails talent, companies, and project owners from around the world." It went on to list sponsors, a schedule of events, and people involved in organizing the "exciting" conference.

Scott said, "Maybe he's the guy mentioned here. Rupert Brown, official photographer."

"It's worth a shot."

There was nothing else to go on, so I copied Rupert's contact details off the brochure, thanked Scott for his help, and went downstairs to give Rupert a call.

TWELVE

R upert answered the phone after two rings.

"This is Gloria Smith," I told him. "I'm one of the organizers of RubyConf, where you helped out?"

"Um, yes?"

He sounded hesitant, but I pressed on. "We've had a great response to the photos you took, and one of our sponsors gave us a free Nikon DSLR camera. I was wondering if you'd like to have it? For free, of course."

I was a bit surprised when he took more than a few seconds to respond. I would've jumped on the offer straight away, but I guess he couldn't remember any Gloria Smith and was a bit skeptical of the whole thing.

"Great," I said, after he agreed to take it. "What's your address? I'll drop it off."

There was another pause. Finally, he said, "4B, 1565 Balzar Avenue."

"Thanks," I said, sounding far more cheerful than I felt. "I'll stop by in a few minutes."

Balzar Avenue is a not-so-nice neighborhood just north-east of the Strip. Houses along the street have thick iron bars on their windows and heavy locks on their front doors. I hadn't been looking forward to meeting Rupert, and now I wasn't looking forward to going to his house. I wondered if there hadn't been some way to trick him into coming out to meet me, but I didn't think he'd willingly co-operate in investigating Crystal's murder.

So I took a deep breath, and walked back to my condo.

I didn't see any new envelopes when I opened my door, which made me feel a tiny bit better, but not much. Someone who lived in Balzar Avenue didn't just secure their property; they learned how to get through that neighborhood at night, which meant they were either tough and strong, or armed. Or both.

I packed my bag for the visit to Rupert's with that in mind. I found my gun and my pepper spray, and stuffed them in. I don't have a permit to carry concealed yet, and I wasn't sure how much they'd help if Rupert was dangerous, but it was worth a shot.

1565 Balzar Avenue turned out to be a large block of boring apartments. There was a massive carpark in front, and a number of cars were still parked there. The building itself looked like it'd been built during the 1970s, and was two stories high with a red brick facade. I climbed up the stairs, and rang the bell to number 4B.

Rupert answered the door and peered out at me. Up close, he didn't seem particularly menacing, and bore an expression hovering between suspicion and hope. His face still had traces of baby fat, and his blue eyes and wispy hair made him look slightly immature. He was wearing khaki shorts and a baby-blue t-shirt, and as far as I could see, he wasn't carrying a gun.

I could see bits of the apartment through the open door – the entrance opened into a small living area, and a hallway veered off behind it, presumably leading to the bedroom and bathroom. There was a couch just to my left, with hoodies, socks and t-shirts strewn all over it, and a coffee table decorated with two used bowls and a mug.

"You're Gloria?" Rupert asked warily, and I smiled.

"Yes."

"Where's the camera?"

"Um," I said. "I didn't actually bring it."

Rupert frowned. "What do you want, then? I'm not buying anything, and I don't have any money to donate."

I took a deep breath, fished a business card out of my bag and handed it over to him. "I'm a private investigator. I was hoping I could ask you a few questions?"

Rupert stared at the card and then up at me. His eyes looked a bit wider, and some of the blood seemed to have drained from his face.

"It's about Crystal Macombe," I told him, and he shook his head.

"There's nothing to talk about."

He moved forward to close the door, and I smiled. "Maybe you'd rather talk to the cops? I can give them the photos you took of her."

He froze and looked at me, and then looked down at my card. "She's dead. Why are you bothering me about her?"

"Did you kill her?"

The question came out more abruptly than I'd intended, and we stared at each other. And then Rupert shook his head. "No, of course not. Why would I kill her?"

"Oh, I don't know. Why don't you tell me?"

He crossed his arms and looked at me belligerently. "I didn't kill her."

"Then maybe you can tell me why you were stalking her."

"I wasn't stalking her."

"You took those photos of her. I've got proof."

"I wasn't stalking her."

I sighed. "I just told you I've got proof. I might as well give the cops the video of you stalking her."

We stared at each other for a few seconds, and then Rupert sighed and his shoulders slumped forward.

"Fine," he said. "Come in."

I stepped inside warily, clutching my handbag, prepared to reach for the pepper spray at any second.

Rupert sat down on a black chair opposite the sofa, put his head in his hands and groaned.

"I knew this would happen," he said, more to himself than to me. "I knew something would go wrong."

I used my forefinger and thumb to pick a hoodie off the sofa, and sat down gingerly on the edge. I kept my handbag on my lap and tried to look sympathetic. "What would go wrong?"

Rupert lifted up his head and looked at me. "I just wanted to be a photographer," he said. "Moved down here 'cause apparently there's good money being a convention photographer, and what do I get? Nothing. No jobs, nothing, and I gotta pay the bills waiting tables. I live in a crummy house in a crummy street and I don't know the right people."

I looked around the room I was sitting in. Rupert didn't seem creepy enough to be a stalker, and something was missing in his apartment. The realization hit me just as I was staring at one of the dirty bowls on the coffee table – where was the wall idolizing Crystal? The one with a collage of photos that he'd taken of her, maybe even a few with him inserted into them with Photoshop? His walls were bare except for a calendar featuring kittens playing with yarn.

"Tell me about Crystal," I said. "Why were you stalking her?"

He shook his head. "I wasn't stalking her. Not really."

I pulled out the photos of Crystal that her boyfriend had given me, and handed them over to Rupert. "What were these?"

Rupert looked at them and sighed. "I was just meant to act like a stalker. Crystal found me through my website and gave me a call. She said she was trying to break into Hollywood, and someone told her that a stalker would help her get famous. So that was me. She'd tell people at the Indie Movie Convention that she had a stalker, people would think she'd be a hot actress, she'd get jobs, and I'd get paid."

His eyes were earnest and pleading, but I said, "That doesn't sound very believable."

"I can prove it," he said, standing up quickly, and I found myself getting to my feet and slipping a hand inside my bag to find the pepper spray.

But he didn't come toward me. He headed toward the kitchen instead, and reappeared after a few seconds, pressing buttons on his cell phone. "Listen," he said.

A woman's recorded voice floated out to me from the phone. "Hey, Ru," she said. "Thanks for the photos. I think, like, I don't need any more, so I'll just pay you for these. Bye."

It was creepy, hearing the voice of someone who'd died, and I looked at Rupert.

"She left this message the day after the convention," he said. "And she paid me straight after. I never saw her again, and I've got nothing to do with her death, I swear."

"Lucky you didn't delete that message," I said suspiciously.

He shrugged. "I couldn't find the time to."

"Anyone else know about this?"

"Yeah…the guy who suggested it to her." He frowned and squinted his eyes, trying to remember, and then his face brightened up. "Got it! Sam something. She said he was the director of a movie she was going to work for."

I sighed. So far, his story added up, and I'd just need to check the details with Sam.

Of course, stalking Crystal as a job didn't mean that he hadn't killed her. I said, "Where were you the night Crystal died?"

Rupert snorted. "You mean, do I have an alibi? Sure. I was waiting tables at The BlueFish restaurant till late, and then I had a few drinks at Paris Bar, hoping to meet someone. Everyone at the bar saw me."

"And did you meet anyone?"

He rolled his eyes. "Women like high-rollers, they don't want a guy who waits tables and lives on Balzar Avenue."

I smiled. "Maybe you should live somewhere else."

"Yeah, maybe."

We said goodbye, and I walked out in a rush of exhaled breath, feeling much better once I was sitting in my car with the doors locked. I drove away as fast as I could, thankful that despite what the rest of my life might be like, I didn't have to wait tables and live in a depressing apartment in a depressing neighborhood.

THIRTEEN

Once I got back to my condo, I parked, removed the gun and pepper spray, and walked over to The Tremonte to meet Sam Rampell.

The set looked different now, somehow more chaotic. There were people running around; a fight scene was being shot and a cameraman with a camera dolly was following the actors. I noticed Minnie trying to apply makeup to three different girls at once. Sam stood and watched, alternating between saying things to the cameraman and actors, and putting his hands on his head and looking frustrated.

He nodded when he saw me, and I went over to him and waited silently till the scene was over.

"Can I talk to you in a few minutes?" he said. "I'm just trying to wrap up a few more scenes before the extras have to take off. I'm only paying them for half the day."

"Sure," I said. "I'll talk to the actors who weren't here this morning."

I did that for the next hour or so, and it was mind-numbingly boring. I learnt nothing new, and had to keep introducing myself over and over again. I was getting nowhere, so it was a relief to hear Sam yell, "Take five, people!"

I was at his side quickly, and he smiled at me, the force of his charisma hitting me like a gust of strong wind.

"I'm all yours," he said. "At least for the next five to ten minutes."

I smiled. "Tell me about Crystal."

His brown eyes grew thoughtful, and he stared off at a point behind me. "She was lovely. Gorgeous person, good actor. I knew she'd hit it big, and I wanted my movie to be her first. She could've done so well in Hollywood."

He let out a disappointed sigh and looked back at me.

"If she was so good," I said, "Why not give her a bigger role?"

Sam smiled. "She was good, she just needed to prove herself."

"Do you think anyone might've been jealous of her? Did she have any enemies?"

He looked at me thoughtfully. "I'm not sure. I don't think she was famous enough to have haters, but it's possible. Maybe someone new met her and didn't like that she'd get a role here."

I nodded. So far, everyone I'd talked to on the set seemed to either have liked Crystal or been unaware of her existence, but maybe someone at the strip club had learnt of her new role and become jealous.

"How about you?" I said. "Do you have any haters?"

Sam smiled. "Just about everyone on set hates me. I'm the director, it's my job to be hated."

I couldn't help liking this guy. "I talked to a guy named Rupert today. Know him?"

Sam squinted at me and shook his head, no.

"He's a photographer. Maybe you forgot his name – he said Crystal hired him to take her photos? Pretend to be a stalker?"

"Ah, yes." Realization dawned on Sam's face. "I remember that thing."

"Oh, so you knew about it?"

"Yeah." He smiled wryly. "Who d'you think gave Crystal the idea?"

I nodded. "So he was just a hired hand."

"Essentially. I knew Crystal could be big, but she needed to build up buzz."

"Then why was he fired after just one set of photos?"

Sam shrugged. "Crystal got what she wanted. I told her it was better to have a stalker here, briefly, and then hire someone again once the movie came out."

"Hmm." I looked at him thoughtfully. It kind of made sense. Well, not really. I didn't get all this Hollywood business, but it was clear that Rupert didn't have anything to do with the murder.

Sam looked at his watch. "Did you have any other questions? I'd like to grab a drink and get back to work, if you're done."

"Oh yeah, I understand. One other thing, where were you that night?"

Sam looked at me, puzzled, and then he smiled. "You mean like my alibi?" He chuckled. "The detective I talked to asked me the same thing. I was out at dinner with Jack and Ben, the producers, and then we hit up a bar and had some drinks."

He was smiling, but I was worried that my question might've offended him, so I said, "Thanks, I'm asking everyone that, so I hope you don't mind."

"Not all. Give me a buzz if you want to ask me anything else, I'm happy to help."

He handed me his card and signaled a waitress, and I went to say hi to Minnie. She was busy giving a guy a real-looking black eye, and I showed her my list of names. There was a tick beside the names of everyone I'd talked to, and there were only a few names without ticks now.

"Seems like you're being really thorough," Minnie told me. "I saw you earlier, shuttling from one person to another."

"Yeah." I nodded. "Big help that's been, though. No-one here knows anything."

"It was worth a shot," Minnie said. "Hope you find out something."

We said goodbye and I headed home. So far, the Hollywood side of Crystal's life hadn't turned up anything, and I wondered if her secret stripper life might turn up something. There was still that pile of mail Max had given me, and though I hate paperwork, I figured it was time to go through it and find out if it held any secrets.

FOURTEEN

I stopped by Glenn's apartment on my way home, and handed him the sprinkles I'd picked up for him the other day.

"You're just in time," he told me. "I've made a big batch of triple-chocolate cupcakes, they're a bit too sugary but I think you'll like them."

"I think I'll *love* them," I said. "No such thing as 'too' sugary."

"Wait here and I'll get them for you. And my lady friend's here, too, so now you can meet her."

Glenn took the sprinkles from me and disappeared. He returned in a few minutes, holding a big plastic box that I knew contained at least a half-dozen big cupcakes, a woman at his side.

"These are for you," he told me, handing over the box.

I peered inside. Big, dark cupcakes, looking and smelling delicious. I smiled.

"Namaste," the woman was saying, and I looked up.

I'd been so blinded by the cupcakes that I'd completely ignored her, and I felt mortified by my rudeness.

"I'm sorry," I said, "I got distracted by these."

I lifted the box to indicate, and looked at her carefully, trying not to appear judgmental.

Glenn's girlfriend wasn't the vacuous twenty-something-year-old I'd expected. I pegged her at about fifty, maybe late fifties. She looked like an aging flower-child, with hip-length brown hair streaked with grey, a floor-length gypsy skirt, and a white t-shirt that showed off her slender figure. She wore no makeup, her pale skin was wrinkled, and her cornflower-blue eyes were smiling at me.

"You must be Tiffany," she said. "I'm Karma."

"Oh?" My eyebrows shot up a little. "I always expected Karma to look different."

She smiled, refusing to take offense, and said, "I get that a lot."

I felt ashamed of my jab immediately, and said, "So that's really your name? Your parents named you Karma?"

"Oh no, they named me Kristine. I changed it to Karma as soon as I could."

"It must've seemed like a good idea at the time." I tried not to sound too disapproving. We all do crazy things when we're young.

"Oh, it was a great idea," Karma said. "I've been blessed – or should I say cursed – with second sight. It's happened through my years of transcendental meditation."

"Uh-huh." I nodded politely and glanced at Glenn, who was smiling. I remembered his admonition to be nice, and said to Karma, "That must come in handy."

"Yes." She nodded. "For instance, that's how I met Glenn. You see, I had a strong sense that something good would happen if I moved into this building."

"You mean, beyond the cheap rent and closeness to the Strip?"

She laughed, a light, tinkling laugh. "I see you're a skeptic."

"What gave that away?" I tried to hide my annoyance behind a polite smile.

Karma leaned forward and looked into my eyes. "I see things in your life, too. You have a darkness in your life, and danger in your future."

"See that, Tiffany?" Glenn said. "Isn't that spot on?" He turned to Karma. "Tiffany's a private investigator. She deals with danger all the time."

I said, "I could've been an accountant with a sexually troubled past, and an angry boss."

Karma smiled. "You'll see. Someday you'll believe me. Just as someday you'll understand that what you're holding there in that box is poison. Sugar will kill you slowly from the inside."

I frowned, unable to help myself. Crazies, I can deal with. Insults to me, I can understand. But how dare she insult Glenn's cupcakes?

I bit back a response, turned to Glenn and said lightly, "Can I speak to you outside for a second, please?"

"I'll be back, honey," he said to Karma, and kissed her lightly on the lips.

"I'll miss you," she called, as he stepped out into the hall with me and closed the door behind himself.

I walked a few paces toward the elevator with Glenn, and then turned to face him.

Before I could say anything, he put up his hands and said, "I warned you she was a bit different."

"But why are you *dating* her? She's nuts!"

Glenn shook his head. "She's not nuts, she's just very talented. And you know, she really can predict things. She saw things in my past that I hadn't told her."

I rolled my eyes. I didn't care if the woman was pretending to be a psychic. What I cared about was that she was dating Glenn.

"Why her?" I asked. "Can't you date someone normal?" Glenn looked offended, and I immediately added, "I'm just concerned for you."

"Well, don't be. I'm doing fine."

I placed my hand on Glenn's forearm and said, "I'm sorry, I do want you to be happy."

Glenn smiled. "It's ok. Besides, aren't you happy she doesn't like sugar? If she did, there'd be fewer cupcakes for you."

"You're right," I said thoughtfully. "I'm glad she thinks sugar is poison."

We said our goodbyes, and I headed up to my condo. Even the delicious-looking cupcakes couldn't displace my concern about Karma. I'm sure she didn't mean any harm, but I worried that she might turn Glenn off sugar too, or maybe hurt him somehow.

I was so engrossed in thinking about Karma as I unlocked my door and opened it, that I almost missed the white envelope lying in the middle of the floor.

It was right there, staring up at me benignly, and I closed my eyes and took a deep breath. My condo was cool, despite the Vegas heat outside, and I'd drawn the curtains before leaving, so it was slightly dark. I opened my eyes again and held my breath, waiting to see if I could hear anything – any noises out of the ordinary. There was the dripping of the bathroom tap, and the drone of a TV next door, but no muffled psychopathic giggling or quiet breathing.

There was probably nobody inside, but I still walked through the room quietly, up to the bedroom door and peeked inside. It was dark and empty. I checked through the bedroom, under the bed, inside the closet, behind the curtains and inside the bathroom. Nobody.

The pounding in my chest began to slow down a little, and I gulped. I walked back to the front door, closed it, and sat down weakly on my sofa. I remembered Karma telling me that I would have danger in my future. I cursed Glen silently for dating her, and wished I'd never met the woman.

The box of cupcakes was sitting on the coffee table in front of me, and I snapped it open and gobbled one down. It was delicious, moist and chocolatey. I was feeling a bit better, so I ate another one. Better still. I was debating whether to eat one more, but then I remembered that I had a party tonight, and I might as well try to save some space for the free food.

I looked at the envelope lying on the floor again and took a deep breath. I might as well get it over with. I was just about to pick it up when my cellphone rang loudly, shattering the quiet.

I sat up straighter, and my heart started pounding loudly again. It's just a phone call, I told myself, and pulled the phone out of my bag.

The caller ID said "Emily" and I answered it nervously.

"Are you ok?" Emily said. "You sound funny."

"I'm fine." I took a deep breath, and then exhaled. I just needed to remember to breathe, that was all.

"I'm calling about those prints. On the photos and that message?"

My ears perked up eagerly. "Yeah?"

"I'm afraid I have bad news."

I frowned. "How bad?"

"There aren't any."

We were both silent for a few seconds, and then I said, "No prints? None at all?"

"None at all." Emily paused and then said, "Whoever sent them must've been wearing gloves. They were very careful."

"Oh." I tried not to think about what that meant, and I glanced at the box of cupcakes. I needed to stay calm. Now was *not* the time to panic. Maybe later I'd panic, but not now.

"You ok? Hello?"

"Yeah, hi. Well, it's good to know that someone *careful* is stalking me." I didn't feel as glib and lighthearted as I sounded. But maybe if I faked it, I'd feel it soon.

"Be careful, Tiff." Emily sounded like she was frowning. "Don't do anything stupid."

"I never do anything stupid," I said. "Thanks for telling me about the prints."

We hung up, and I looked at the envelope again. Somehow it seemed more menacing now, mocking me with its blank, fingerprints-less whiteness.

"You can have more cupcakes once you get see what's in there," I told myself, and the bribe worked. I opened the envelope.

At first, there were just more photos of me. Me meeting Stone, eating my burger and talking to Stone. Walking up to The Tremonte, entering The MontePatria Casino, heading back to my condo.

There were a *lot* of photos of me. I wondered how I'd missed the photographer, considering that I'd been looking over my shoulder every five minutes or so. But it's easy to get lost in a crowd of snap-happy tourists, and these snaps were probably taken with a telephoto lens.

At the end of the snapshots, there were a couple more photos of me, my face blown up to almost fill the whole frame — but this time the guy had gotten a bit more creative, and had used photo editing software to add in a knife held against my throat. Any other time, I would've laughed – the photo manipulation was amateurish, and the knife didn't look very realistic. But this wasn't any other time, and I frowned and bit my lip. I didn't like where this was going, and even though he wasn't good with Photoshop, the guy had made his point.

And just to rub in that point, after the creative pictures there was a piece of paper with a one-line message on it: "You'll never know when."

I ate two more cupcakes but they just made me feel sick. Maybe Karma was right, maybe what I'd just eaten was poison.

I sat curled up against my ratty sofa for some time, not liking how I was feeling, trying not to think about the message, but in the end I picked up my phone and tried to stop my fingers trembling long enough to call Stone.

I told him about the new envelope, and he was silent for so long that I thought maybe he'd hung up. But then he said, "Has Emily gotten back to you about the prints?"

"No go. The guy must've been wearing gloves."

Stone swore softly. "I was hoping we'd get prints."

"It's a minor setback," I said lightly. "He can't always be careful."

On the other end of the line, Stone was silent again.

"You could say something to cheer me up," I suggested, but Stone was still silent.

Finally, he said, "I can't always be there, so I'll get one of my guys to stick with you from now on."

I appreciated the concern, but I didn't like feeling dependent on Stone—especially when I wasn't paying for his services—so, of course, like an idiot, I said, "No, it's fine. I can take care of myself."

There was a brief second of silence, and then Stone said, "I'm coming round at seven, are you stepping out before then?"

"No."

"Ok."

He hung up, and I ate another cupcake, appetite for dinner be damned.

I took a hot shower, found a dress to wear to the dinner, made my bed and vacuumed the condo. Finally, when I ran out of other things to procrastinate with, I sat down with the papers Max had given me.

There was a notebook among the papers, and I pulled that out first. I was hoping it'd be a diary, detailing all of Crystal's secrets and shedding light on the murder, but it turned out to be a day planner. It could still be useful, I told myself, and flipped through the pages. It was completely blank.

I took a deep breath and tried to stop myself from throwing the empty day planner at the door. Maybe someone had given the day planner to Crystal, maybe she thought it made her look more successful, or maybe she carried it around hoping its organizational skills would transfer over to her through osmosis. Either way, it was zero help to me.

Next, I sorted through all the papers. There were bills and bank statements, copies of Crystal's resume, a file containing large, professional photos of Crystal, a postcard, and a photo of a chubbier, older version of Crystal with three kids and a man with a receding hairline. I figured that was Crystal's sister Carol, with her kids and husband.

I went through Crystal's resume with an ironic smile. She'd gone to high school in Nebraska, and then moved straight to

LA. She'd been a waitress for a while, but she'd quit that job two years ago. I guessed that was when she discovered the profitability of being a stripper. I noticed she'd also had roles as an extra in three movies, two of which had been directed by Sam Rampell. That's probably how he'd noticed her, and decided to give her a minor speaking role in Casino Kings.

There were two bills – one from the Screen Actors' Guild, informing Crystal that her fees were due, and a copy of her cellphone bill. Neither of these told me much, other than the fact that Crystal was part of the SAG, and that she had an expensive, latest-model cellphone which she used pretty frequently.

The bank statement covered the last three months, and I went through it carefully. There were once-a-month deposits, a couple of grand each time, which I assumed was her income from being a stripper. Other than those deposits, there was no money coming in. There were a couple of cash withdrawals, and there was a regular, once-a-month bank transfer of five thousand dollars each month, for the last three months, to a Cheryl Czekanski.

Cheryl must've been one hell of a pal for Crystal to transfer so much money over to her each month, but I'd never heard of this girl's name before. I switched on my laptop and typed it in, half-hoping that I'd find a result. Instead, there were twenty pages of results. Clearly, there was a large population of Polish women named Cheryl, so I changed my search to "Cheryl Czekanski, Las Vegas."

This time, I got about five pages of results. I clicked through the top couple of results – there was a dermatologist, a marketing expert, a nutritionist. This was going nowhere. I skipped over to the "Image" results, hoping I'd see a familiar face. Once again, I didn't see anyone I recognized. There were photos of the dermatologist, the marketing expert and the nutritionist, along with photos of a dozen other girls. There were a couple of kids who looked about five years old, and I had a brief moment of worry about their privacy before I moved on. There was a photo of a gorgeous blonde, a woman with curly black hair, and someone who wore two-inch thick eyeliner and had dyed her hair purple.

I switched off my laptop and called Samantha. My phone went straight to voicemail, so I assumed she was at work and left her a message, letting her know I'd come by to talk to her tomorrow. I needed to talk to Crystal's friends at The Peacock Bar, and maybe I could ask Samantha if she knew Cheryl Czekanski.

It was almost time for the party, so I slipped into the shimmery green dress I'd selected, piled on some eyeliner, mascara and lipstick, and ran a straightener through my hair till I figured I could almost pass as an extremely high-class escort.

There was a knock on my door at exactly seven, and I wondered whether Stone had arrived early and waited in his car until the precise, correct time. When I opened the door, he raised one eyebrow almost imperceptibly, and I thought I saw the hint of a smile.

"I've never seen you wearing a dress before," he said.

"And I've never seen you wearing a suit."

Our eyes met and held for a brief second. I wondered whether I should admit that he looked good, but I waited for him to say something first. Another second ticked away.

Finally, I said, "Aren't you going to tell me I look nice?"

Stone smiled. "I knew you'd say that."

I scowled and grabbed my bag, feeling as though I'd lost in some childish game. "Why can't you act like an adult?" I grumbled as we approached the elevator.

"Why can't you?"

Trouble is, I *was* acting like an adult. That's why I wanted him to compliment me, and that's why I thought he looked like James Bond but couldn't say anything about it. Sure, James Bond drives an Aston Martin, and Stone drives a silver Porsche convertible, but I'm pretty sure the similarities end there.

I stepped into his car and placed my tiny, beaded purse on my lap. The engine purred into life, and just before he pulled away from the curb, Stone reached over and grabbed my hand in his.

My skin seemed to burn where he touched me, and I felt a jolt of electricity run up my arm and spread through my body. I looked at him in surprise. His eyes had softened and he said gently, "You look beautiful."

The air seemed to have left my body and I wondered if he'd lean forward to kiss me. I was beginning to think it might have been a bad idea to invite Stone to the party, when he released my hand and began to drive away.

We didn't say anything on the short drive up to The MontePatria Casino. With anyone else, that might have been awkward, but I was used to being in silence next to Stone. Still, I wondered if I'd misread something in our conversation there.

———

OUTSIDE THE FORUM Ballroom, where the party was being held, there were two men with square bodies stuffed into dark suits, checking everyone's invitation cards.

Stone and I slid past them effortlessly, and once we were inside, I took a moment to imbibe the atmosphere. Like most places in Vegas, the room was large and ostentatious. Massive chandeliers hung from the ceiling, Romanesque art hung from the walls, and the floor was varicolored marble. The lighting was diffused and classy, and I thought I heard the subtle notes of classical music above the low hum of polite conversation.

The women were all dressed in slinky outfits like mine, and the men were in suits or tuxedos. Everyone was sipping drinks and nibbling hors d'oeuvres elegantly. There was an air of chummy belongingness inside the room – everyone here was wealthy, powerful, or important, or all three. Except for Stone and myself, of course. And I'm not really sure about Stone – for all I knew, he was wealthy and successful, and a powerful behind-the-scenes advisor to some bigshots.

I glanced around the room, trying to find a man who matched the photos of Jeremy, the owner of the stolen Van Gogh, that Stacey had shown me. There were only a hundred or so people, and I spotted Jeremy right away – he was holding a glass of whisky in his hand and chatting with two women in their late sixties.

I nudged Stone. "That's him."

We began to walk over to Jeremy when Stone ran into someone he knew.

"You son-of-a-bitch!" the chubby, grey-haired man said. "Good to see you again!"

"Harry."

They did some back-slappingly manly hugging, and then Stone introduced me. "This is Harry," he told me. "I did some work for him."

"Are you kidding?" the man said. "Guy practically saved my business. And me."

Stone asked how Noel and Sharon were doing, and they chatted about these mysterious people for a few minutes before we moved on. Jeremy was alone now, glancing vaguely at the guests and probably looking for someone he knew.

We were about to make a beeline for him, when Detective Elwood stepped in front of me, blocking our path.

"Tiffany Black," he said slowly, "How nice to see you here."

Elwood's voice was low, and I seemed to detect a slightly menacing edge. He looked incongruous in his shiny, slightly-too-tight suit, and in his left hand he held a glass of transparent liquid with a slice of lime in it. To the casual observer, it looked like a vodka tonic, but as an experienced dealer, I know a decoy drink when I see one – it was definitely a club soda, and he was definitely not drinking.

He nodded at Stone and said, "I wish I could say it's a pleasure meeting you."

"I wish I could say the same," Stone replied.

A waitress passed by with a tray of smoked salmon topped with crème fraiche and chives on thin crackers, and Elwood grabbed one for himself. "What're you doing here?" he asked Stone.

"Business," Stone said.

Elwood snorted. "I'll bet. As long as it's nothing we have to look into later."

Before Stone could reply, Elwood turned to me and said, "Why am I not surprised to see you two together?"

I looked at him in disbelief. "How do you mean?" He just snorted again, and I said, "What're *you* doing here?"

He inhaled the cracker in one bite and narrowed his eyes. "I've got a hunch that whoever stole the Van Gogh is gonna turn up here. Lots of art lovers. You can't sell it on the black market or through a dealer, now that we're investigating, but you *can* sell one on one. This party is just an excuse for introductions."

He glanced at Stone and then back at me again. "Let me know if you meet anyone interesting."

Elwood walked away, trying to chase down a waitress carrying a tray of exotic-looking mini-sandwiches, and Stone and I looked at each other.

"Man's a nutcase," I said.

Stone nodded. "Amazing how a woman can screw you up like that."

He gave me a long look and I said, "Hey! It's not like women collude together to screw up men. Men do it to themselves."

"Hmm."

We looked around, trying to find Jeremy, but he was nowhere to be seen.

"Oh crap!" I said. "Don't tell me he's left already?"

"Impossible. Everyone stays for the speeches."

I frowned. What would I tell Stacey, that I'd lost the man in the middle of a crowded room? I looked back at Elwood, who'd managed to chase down the waitress, and was now stuffing his face with whatever she had on her tray, and cursed him silently.

There were three tall, roundish men in their early sixties standing in front of us, all wearing boots and cowboy hats. They were laughing about something and I pegged them as Texans.

"Well, nice meeting you," one of them said, "I'm gonna find me another drink. How 'bout you, fellas?"

The other two aging cowboys agreed that they, too, wanted drinks. All three of them spotted a waitress carrying a tray of champagne glasses at the same time, and they all wandered off after her.

That's when I saw Jeremy. The three Texans had been talking to him, shielding him from our view with their wide hats and even wider bodies. I felt a wave of relief wash through me, and Stone and I sauntered up to him.

"Hi," Stone said, "We haven't met. I'm Jonathon Stone, and this is Tiffany."

"Jeremy."

We shook hands and Stone asked some polite questions – what brought him here? Did he know Oscar Goodman personally? Weren't the tourists being awful this year?

I'd always thought of Stone as being a silent, stoic person, so seeing him turn on the charm was a bit of a surprise. In contrast, I felt like an awkward, frizzy-haired teenager, not quite knowing what to say.

After a while, Jeremy asked Stone what he did, and he used this opportunity to pull out his card and hand it over. "Security services, mainly," Stone said. "Plus some investing, some funding new companies."

"Sounds interesting," Jeremy said. "I'm involved with clothing imports."

I racked my brains to come up with some way of talking about the theft, but I couldn't. Stone said, "Oh, that's a guy I have to say hello to over there. I'll catch you guys later."

He disappeared, and I shifted my weight uncomfortably. "So," I said. "Do you travel much?"

Jeremy shrugged. "Just a bit for business."

He clearly wasn't about to bring up the theft on his own so I said, "Yeah. I've got a friend working insurance, says thefts really go up when people leave town."

"Oh?" Jeremy began looking around, clearly trying to escape, and I cursed my conversational skills. Usually they're quite good – except when it really matters.

"Yeah." I nodded. "She's working on this one theft now, guy lived in Ascend Towers and his Van Gogh was stolen."

Jeremy's attention switched back to me with laser-precision. "Really? What else did she say?"

"Uh...She just said to travel safe."

I was mentally slapping my forehead. How had I gotten so stuck? I would've been better off even if I'd just asked him straight up, "Hey, I heard you got your painting stolen. Any idea who did it?"

Instead, here I was, being pumped for information by Jeremy.

He said, "What about this Van Gogh theft? Are they working on it?"

I frowned, trying to think fast. "I guess I shouldn't talk about. It could be anyone here."

We looked at each other warily. This conversation was going downhill fast, and I needed to do some damage control. "Actually," I said, "She told me that the guy who owned the painting was called Jeremy. Is that you?"

We stared at each other in silence, and then he said, "Yeah, it is me, actually."

I could see him trying to figure out if I'd known all along that it'd been his painting, so I quickly said, "Wow, what a coincidence! Small world, huh?"

He smiled a terse, tight-lipped smile, not seeming to have been convinced by my act, but I pressed on. "I'm so sorry about the robbery. It must feel awful."

"Yeah," he said. "It's pretty awful."

"Any idea who did it? Or how it happened?"

He shrugged. "Just some guy, I guess."

"But I heard you've got great security at Ascend. How'd he get through?"

"Umm, I'm not sure really."

"Security must've been off?"

"Yeah, I think he turned it off. Anyway…"

He was trying to run off again, so I said, "Geez, I hope the insurance pays out properly."

Jeremy focused his attention on me again and said, "Why, did your friend say anything?"

I frowned and thought back to what Stacey had said. "I think they're meant to pay out after three months, right? Unless it turns up again."

He nodded. "That's what they say. Those scum better pay up, this time."

He glanced over my shoulder, nodded at someone and said, "I should go say hi to my friend, over there."

I followed his glance and almost stopped breathing. His "friend" was Green Eyes.

FIFTEEN

O f course, I wasn't completely sure he was the man I'd seen falling from the sky that day, but he was definitely the man I'd seen in The Tremonte that night. The man who'd disappeared into thin air. Our eyes had met and Green Eyes was smiling at me now, and I held his glance and smiled back. There was no way, no way on Earth that he'd disappear on me a third time.

"It was lovely meeting you," Jeremy was saying, and I snapped back to reality.

"Yes, you too," I heard myself saying automatically. "Is that your friend over there? He looks kind of familiar, I might've met him somewhere. Could you introduce me to him, please?"

Jeremy looked at me, trying to keep the exasperation out of his eyes. I was *that* person. The leech. The one who meets you at a party and sticks to you like superglue, the one whose sole aim in life seems to be to prevent you from having a good time.

"Um…" He was clearly trying to think of an excuse to not introduce me.

"Please?" I said. "The only other person I know here is the guy I came with, and he's gone off somewhere. I'd love to meet your friend!"

I didn't care about dignity or pride or self-respect. All I cared about was sticking to Jeremy and meeting Green Eyes.

I could see the annoyance start to show through the edges of Jeremy's carefully composed expression. But it was a hard request to turn down, and Green Eyes was already heading right for us.

"Sure," he said.

I tried not to grin too broadly, and we took a few steps forward.

"Jack," said Jeremy, "This is Tiffany Black. Tiffany, Jack Weber."

We smiled at each other. His eyes were green, flecked with tiny bits of gold, and his forehead was broad with strands of dark hair falling over the sides. I felt myself start to get lost in his eyes and quickly said, "It's nice to meet you."

"You, too," he said.

I wondered if he meant it. But he looked genuinely interested in talking to me, and this time he hadn't run off. I decided that I wasn't going to make the same mistake I'd made when talking to Jeremy, and I jumped straight in. "Didn't I see you at The Tremonte the other night?"

The corners of his mouth went up a little. "It's possible. I'm there quite often."

"Oh? Why is that?"

He looked amused, and said, "I own half the place."

"Oh."

I felt like an idiot and was trying to think of something polite to say. It annoyed me that his mysterious disappearance, and the security guy's refusal to talk about him, were both explained away so easily.

Jack said, "Your name sounds familiar. Have we met before?"

I narrowed my eyes. *I* wanted to be the one asking if we'd met before.

"I remember!" Jack said, recognition dawning on his face. "You did some work for Sophia Becker, right?"

I tried not to look completely stunned. "How do you know Sophia?"

"I bought off her shares of The Riverbelle."

"That must've made her sister-in-law mad."

We smiled at each other, and Jeremy turned to me and said, "What work did you do for Sophia?"

I felt my mind go blank and I began mumbling, trying to think of something to say.

"She's a private investigator," Jack said to him. "And she's really good."

Jeremy glared at me. "So AAI sent you, huh?"

"Uh…"

"I don't know how you live with yourself," he hissed.

His hostility surprised me, but before I could say anything, he turned and huffed away.

Jack looked amused.

"What was that about?" I asked him.

He looked at me thoughtfully. "Lucky I remembered you're a PI. So, you're working for AAI, huh?"

"Um, not really."

I glanced around the room, wondering where Stone was. There was a group of about half a dozen men huddled in one corner of the room, talking and laughing, and when one of them moved away, I noticed that the ex-mayor was a part of the group, and Stone was saying something that made him laugh uproariously.

Jack followed my glance and then turned his attention back to me. "So, what brings you here?"

I looked back at him. "I could ask you the same thing."

He shrugged. "I gave the guy a donation once, so now I'm invited to these things. But how does a PI get an invitation to this, and more specifically, why?"

His eyes were smirking silently, a mixture of amusement and curiosity, and I tried to think of something to say that would change the topic. His name sounded vaguely familiar – Jack Weber. Where had I heard that before?

I remembered and looked at him in surprise. "You're the co-producer of Casino Kings."

He raised an eyebrow. "Yes."

"Your name was on the list Tony gave me," I explained, but he just looked more puzzled. "I'm investigating Crystal Macombe's death. She had a role in Casino Kings."

"Oh. I *think* Sam mentioned wanting to hire someone to replace Sally. But I didn't know her name was Crystal, or that she died."

"You're not a very hands-on producer, are you?"

He grinned and shook his head.

"Then why bother?" I asked. "Doesn't The Tremonte keep you busy enough? And you own part of The Riverbelle, too."

He smiled. "Casinos are boring. Business is all about money and profitability and looking at operations." He shrugged. "I thought the movie world might be a bit more interesting."

If I were a multi-million dollar businessman who owned large shares in large casinos, I'd probably be happy with my life and not complain about boredom. But then again, what do I know about being a casino owner? Maybe Jack's life was one big sob story.

"And how'd that turn out?" I said. "You don't even know what's going on in your own movie."

He smiled again. "Yes, but word gets around there's a guy wanting to throw money at movies, all kinds of people start wanting to be your friend. Very *int-eresting* people."

I tried to keep my face expressionless, but all I could think of was, *pig*. He was probably doing this to meet beautiful actresses. I couldn't stop myself from imagining him standing arm in arm with Angelina Jolie, talking and laughing about something. A wave of jealousy hit me like a punch in the stomach. I couldn't compete with Angelina. Not even if I gave up cupcakes forever and spent half my life at the gym. *Pig*.

"Why are you frowning?" Jack said. "What pig?"

I snapped out of my reverie. "Huh?"

"You said 'pig.' You weren't calling me a pig, were you?"

I looked at him blankly. "No, of course not."

Jack seemed amused. "You think I'm a pig because I'm financing movies to meet women?"

It sounded absurd when he said it out loud. "No, of course not," I repeated. Jack continued to look amused, and I could feel myself blushing. "I, uh, was thinking of that charity where you buy pigs for poor people."

"Which charity?"

"The Pig Foundation."

"Right."

Jack was smiling broadly, and looked like he was trying not to laugh. I quickly added, "I'm not sure if they exist anymore, but they used to do really good work." I was babbling, and I needed to change the topic before I made a bigger fool of myself. I tried to push my brain to think faster. Bingo! "What do you think of the other people working on the movie?"

His smile disappeared immediately, and I patted myself of the back. Sure, my thoughts might inadvertently turn into speech sometimes, but I'm still able to change the topic in time.

"Do you think Crystal's death might have something to do with the movie?" he asked, and I shook my head.

"I'm not sure yet, I'm looking into everything. Did you ever meet Crystal?"

"No. Financing movies is as boring as any other business. I just know the other producer Ben, and the director and screenwriter."

"What d'you think of them?"

"Jack!" said a voice so loud and deep I was surprised it hadn't caused an earthquake. "We've been looking all over for you!"

The voice was behind me, so I turned around. It belonged to one of the Texans, and his two buddies were right beside him.

I turned to look back at Jack. His expression was one of studied politeness, and he said, "Good to see you, Bart. And you too, Mike; Eddie."

The Texan trio began shaking hands with Jack, and saying something about the weather in Vegas and the last time they were down here…

I was about to ease my way out, when Jack fished out a business card and wrote down something on the back.

"That's my private number on the back," he said, handing me the card. "Give me a call and we'll talk about the movie."

The Texans glanced at me curiously, obviously wondering if I was a movie star or executive. I'm sure they decided on the latter, because their glances weren't *that* curious.

"Jack," one of them boomed, "Aren't you going to introduce us to your beautiful friend?"

I smiled. Despite their booming voices and their outfits, these men still knew chivalry.

Introductions were made, and I excused myself, not seeing the point of hanging around any longer. My job at the party was done. Almost. All that was left for me to do was snag a couple of hors d'oeuvres, maybe chug a free drink, and then get home for a night in.

"Remember to call me," Jack said, as I left. We smiled at each other and his eyes were so intense that I had to remind myself to breathe.

Of course I'd remember to call him.

SIXTEEN

After I'd guzzled down a glass of expensive white wine and devoured at least a dozen of those fancy mini-sandwiches and nibbles-on-a-stick, Stone and I headed home.

"That was a pretty good party," I said.

Stone nodded, and I waited for him to say something. I'd seen him shaking hands and chatting with people, while I'd spent most of my time being the typical wallflower, albeit one who ate a lot.

He didn't say anything, so I prompted, "Did you meet anyone interesting?"

"Did you?"

He focused his glance on me, and I knew he'd seen me chatting with Jack.

I shrugged. "Just work stuff."

I didn't feel like talking about Jack, and we drove the rest of the way in silence. There seemed to be something in the air, something bordering on awkwardness, and I didn't feel like exploring what it was.

"I'll walk you up," Stone said, parking near my condo.

"No, I'll be fine."

He ignored me and we rode up in the elevator together, our usual comfortable silence not feeling quite right.

"I'm stopping by Glenn's," I told him. "He said he'd do some baking today."

There was no response from Stone, but he followed me out and waited as I knocked on Glenn's door.

Karma answered the door. She was wearing a bright orange turban, and a flowing, white maxi-dress that looked kind of like a nightgown. Her eyes were rimmed with dark kohl and her lips were smeared a reddish-maroon.

"Tiffany!" she said, clutching her chest. "My God, I'm so glad to see you. I thought you were in grave danger."

She ushered us inside, and I saw Glen walking toward us.

I tried not to roll my eyes. "I'm fine," I told her. "I just stopped by to say hi."

Karma peered at Stone and looked at me again. "Maybe this young man is protecting you from the dangers? I sense you two have a close connection. Maybe romantic?"

Glen had reached us by now and he smiled. "Hello, Stone." The two men shook hands. "It's good to see you again."

"You too, sir," Stone said.

"These days, you don't meet very many young men as nice as this one," Glenn told me, and I smiled stiffly.

Karma looked at me carefully, and reached out one hand. She placed the tips of her fingers on the side of my neck, and I tried not to flinch at her feather-light touch.

"Are you two together?" she asked me. "I can sense you have a strong bond."

I did a mental eye-roll and looked at Stone. The corners of his lips had gone up and I knew that he too, was mentally shaking his head.

"We're friends," I told Karma. "We just met a few months ago."

She removed her hand from my neck and waved it, like she was flicking away an imaginary mosquito.

"Time is unimportant," she announced. "It is the connection of the soul that matters."

I nodded slowly. "Ri-ight."

"The spirits tell me there will be romance in your future," Karma said. "But it will be complicated, and might not make you happy."

"Oh." My stomach felt funny and I frowned. I didn't want to believe in Karma's spirits, and I didn't want to believe in a complicated romance. But maybe the feeling in my stomach was just telling me that I'd had too many fancy hors d'oeuvres. Those tidbits were probably meant to be eaten one at a time, not one handful after another.

"The man will have green eyes," Karma continued, and my eyes widened. "Do you know a man with green eyes?"

I shook my head furiously, unwilling to tell Karma about Jack, and gulped. Now I wanted to believe her spirits.

Glenn cleared his throat, and looked pointedly at Karma, who looked back at him and sighed.

"Tiffany," Glenn said lightly, "Are you working on a case right now?"

"Yes. Why?"

He was holding a big plastic food container in his hands, and he looked at it and said, "I didn't know you were out, so Karma and I stopped by your place earlier. I wanted to give you this box of cupcakes. They're apple and cinnamon, with vanilla and cinnamon frosting."

I grinned broadly and he gave me the box before I could snatch it out of his hands. "Thanks."

"Um…" Glen glanced at Karma and then looked back at me. "Karma and I saw a man standing outside your door. He looked like he was trying to slip an envelope under your door."

My smile disappeared, and I was conscious of the silence in the air. My hands felt clammy, and there seemed to be a chill somewhere. I felt Stone take a protective step closer to me.

"What did he look like?" I asked Glen.

Glen shook his head. "We don't know. He was wearing a black ski mask."

I felt dizzy. I breathed in deeply and closed my eyes. "What else?"

"Sorry?"

"What else was he wearing?"

I opened my eyes to see Glenn looking a bit puzzled. My question probably made no sense, but all I could think of was Green Eyes wearing the ski mask and suit.

"Jeans, I guess," said Glenn. "Dirty-looking jeans and a gray-ish t-shirt."

I exhaled. It couldn't be Green Eyes – Jack – because I couldn't imagine him not wearing a suit. Unless Jack wasn't Green Eyes. But that couldn't be.

"He had a dark soul," Karma said. "I could sense his evil. He's very angry at you."

"You think?" The words came out unchecked, and I sighed. "I'm sorry, I didn't mean to be sarcastic."

"It's ok," Karma told me. "I understand your fear. But you must be careful."

I looked back at Glenn. "Are you ok? He didn't – threaten you or anything did he?"

Glenn smiled and shook his head. "We're fine, thanks to Karma." He exchanged a happy glance with her and said, "She started screaming at the guy, and then she grabbed the box from my hands and threw it at him. Almost hit him in the face. He ran away through the fire escape."

"I'm glad you're ok," I said, and peeked under the lid of the box at the cupcakes. *They* weren't ok – the icing was all smooshed and some of it was stuck to the sides of the box. I tried not to look disappointed. Glenn was ok, and that's what mattered. Still, Karma didn't have to go around throwing boxes of cupcakes at people.

"He's not a good person," Karma told me, and I bit back the response that came to my mind. "I hope he stays away from you."

"Did you see his eyes?" I asked her, and she nodded.

"Yes, eyes, the windows to the soul. His soul was dark."

I nodded impatiently. "Yes, yes, what *color* were they?"

Karma looked at me, surprised, and I said slowly, "What. Color. Were. His eyes?"

"I told you," she said, "They were dark. Like his soul."

"So not green?"

"No. Dark brown."

I breathed a sigh of relief.

"He ran off with the envelope," Karma continued. "I hope it didn't have an important message in it."

"I'm sure it didn't," I told her. "And we should get going."

"Yes," Stone agreed, and we said our goodbyes and headed up to my apartment.

Stone made me wait outside for a few minutes while he checked through my apartment, and then he gave me the all-clear to come inside.

"That's it," he told me. "I'm going everywhere with you from now on."

"It's fine. I'll be fine."

But my words sounded hollow even to me, and Stone just shook his head and left.

Before I went to bed, I pulled Jack's card out of my tiny purse and smiled to myself.

"Jack Weber," it said, "Entrepreneur."

Short and sweet. And then, like a sudden punch in the face, realization hit me. I knew where else I'd heard that name. He was one of the owners of the red Ferraris, the ones whose number plates matched up. Jack Weber was Green Eyes. I couldn't prove it, but I knew "in my soul," as Karma would say, that he'd stolen the Van Gogh.

As I drifted off to sleep, I thought back to Jack. He was too successful to be a career criminal, and he was too charming for me to believe that he was a thief. But he was involved somehow; I just couldn't put my finger on it.

SEVENTEEN

E arly to bed and early to rise was not something I did very often. But when I do, I feel like a million bucks – not least because I didn't have to spend the previous night dealing with drunk, aggressive gamblers in a too-bright, too-loud casino pit.

So the next morning, I woke up feeling all bright and cheery. I smiled as I remembered the delicious hors d'oeuvres of the previous night, and the way Jack had reminded me to call him. And then I remembered the box of apple-cinnamon cupcakes sitting in my fridge, and I felt even happier. This would be a perfect day. Well, ok, I'd promised my parents that I'd have lunch at their place today; but other than that, it would be a perfect day.

I changed into clean jeans and a white blouse, and started on my breakfast. I'd just finished my first cupcake and half a mug of coffee when my phone rang. I recognized the LVMPD number, and answered, thinking it was Emily.

"This is Elwood," said Detective Elwood's voice. "How are you?"

I stifled a sigh when I heard his voice, and reminded myself that today would be a perfect day.

"Good," I said warily, not bothering to ask how he was. I knew how he was – chugging away on coffee-flavored cream and sugar, pining for his ex-wife.

"Can you come into the precinct?" he asked, and I nodded.

See? I told myself. The perfect day. I'd been meaning to go to the precinct anyway.

"How about in a few minutes from now?" I asked.

"Of course," he said, his voice ridiculously polite. "It's not like I have anything else to do."

I chose to ignore his sarcasm. "Thanks, I'll see you soon."

"Hunh," he said, and hung up.

I shrugged and put the phone away. If he was busy, he'd have said something. Getting this out of the way first thing meant I could spend the rest of the day investigating Crystal's death.

I heard raised voices outside my door, and peered out through the peephole. I couldn't see anything, so I opened the door a crack, and peered around to my left.

Stone was standing in the hallway, typing into his phone and studiously trying to avoid Mrs. Weebly.

"You can't just loiter here," she said. "Visitors can't just loiter."

"I'm waiting for my friend to come out," Stone said, sounding as though he'd been repeating this line quite a few times. He caught my eye and I made a face. Before Mrs. Weebly could step forward, Stone slipped inside my condo and closed the door behind us.

"You can't just leave like that!" Mrs. Weebly yelled, her voice shrill and piercing. "Where are your manners?"

Stone and I looked at each other.

"Did she remember you're my friend?" I asked. "Does she know you're here to visit me?"

Stone rolled his eyes and nodded.

I groaned. "Great. Now she'll bring this up at the HOA meeting. Why couldn't you just knock on my door like a regular guy?"

"Didn't want to wake you."

"Then wait in your car! You don't even have to be here!"

Stone looked at me seriously, and I looked away. I was worried he could see through me, and truth be told, after last night, I was actually looking forward to a bit of company.

"I've got a few hours to be around you," Stone told me. "But after that, you're on your own."

I nodded, not quite sure what to say, and we headed down to the station, Stone driving close behind me.

EIGHTEEN

E lwood was slumped over some papers in front of him, and he only glanced up when I was a few inches from his desk. Stone had gone off to talk to some detective he knew, and I wondered briefly why Elwood seemed to hate him.

"Hard at work?" I asked, smiling, but Elwood refused to smile back.

There was a half a mug of coffee sitting on his desk, and judging from the strange white sheen on top, I guessed it had been sitting there for almost a day now. Elwood looked as grumpy as usual, and his skin looked blotchy with dark circles under his eyes. And then I noticed he was wearing a white shirt, unbuttoned at the collar, and a dark jacket hung over his chair.

"Are you still wearing last night's clothes?" I said. "Don't they let you go home for the night?"

He narrowed his eyes at me. "I happen to be busy."

I nodded. "Lots of big cases?"

He grunted, and I glanced at the mess of papers scattered before him. A brief, flickering thought entered my mind – was he trying to avoid going back home because his wife was no longer there? But I pushed the thought away impatiently. I'd be a typical Vegas sucker if I felt sorry for every loser I met.

"What'd you want to talk about?" I said, trying to move things along.

Elwood stared at me through hooded eyes and I wondered how he functioned as a cop if he was sleep-deprived.

Finally, he said, "Interesting seeing you at the party last night."

I smiled and waited for him to get to the point. He rubbed one eye and said, "I feel like you know something about this theft."

"I think I might. I was going to come here to tell you." Elwood raised one eyebrow and leaned back and I said, "The results of Ferrari license plates. Jack Weber was one of the owners. I think it's him."

"And why's that?"

"I just…" I thought back to his eyes, and the strong "feeling in my soul" about this.

But saying that out loud would make me look like an idiot, so I said, "He's the same height and eye color as the man I saw jump out that building. You *have* to investigate this."

Elwood sighed. "How do you know he's the same height?"

"They look the same."

"Height's a tough thing to guess. Eyes look different colors in different lights, and lots of people have green or blue eyes. Got anything else?"

I looked at him in disbelief. "Don't you think it's at least worth looking into?"

Elwood shook his head. "Do I think it's worth looking into a man who's got a decent alibi and is one of the biggest donors of the LVMPD Foundation? You've got to be nuts."

I crossed my arms. Donating to the LVMPD Foundation was a nice thing to do, but it just made me all the more suspicious of Jack. Nobody donated to the cops unless they had an ulterior motive.

"Any other suspects you want to talk about?" Elwood said. "Maybe the mayor, or the state senator?"

I looked at him, not smiling. "So you're really not going to look into Jack?"

The left side of Elwood's mouth went up in a crooked smile. "I'm not an idiot."

I didn't believe that, but I didn't say anything.

"So," Elwood went on, "Is there anything else you want to tell me?"

"Like what?"

He shrugged. "Oh, I don't know. You're a big-shot PI, you've got lots of contacts and meet people at fancy parties, you tell me."

"Are you asking me to share notes about what I learnt at last night's party?"

He leaned forward. "No. I'm asking you to tell me why you really went to the party. Are you trying to pawn off the Van Gogh? Do you have a buyer in mind?"

I stared at him for a few seconds, and then I shook my head. "Why would I have a buyer?" He continued to look at me intently and my eyes widened. "Oh my God. You don't think I stole it, do you?"

He shook his head. "No, I don't think you're smart enough to steal a Van Gogh. But I think you might know who did it, and you might be helping them sell it off."

I raised my hands, exasperated. "I already told you. Look into Jack Weber."

"Nice try. I'm not falling for that and wasting my time."

I stared at him for a few seconds and sighed. "Why would I even know who stole it?"

"I don't know…seems like you know people. Women like you, getting into private parties, going around escorted by that thug, Stone – first you say you're a dealer, then you tell me you're a PI. I think you really are a dealer, just not a casino dealer."

I stared at him, as though I was seeing his pudgy face for the first time.

"That's crazy," I said softly.

"Is it? Because I don't think it is. I think you're hiding something and I think we'd be better off if you admitted to it."

The sleep deprivation must've addled his brain.

"I've told you everything I know," I said stiffly. "And now I need to get to my appointments."

I stood up and walked out, feeling a bit rattled by the whole thing. Stone joined me silently at the door, walking with me across the car park.

"How'd it go?" he asked me as we walked. "You look funny."

I sighed. "People are nuts."

"That's a generalization," he said. "Different people are different kinds of nuts."

I got into my car and sat there with the engine idling for a few seconds. I didn't like the fact that Elwood thought I knew something or, worse, was an accessory to the crime.

Maybe he'd been bluffing and was trying to get me to tell him something, but I didn't think so. Perhaps he was sleep deprived, and it was making him think crazy thoughts. Or maybe he'd given up on discovering the thief, and was more intent on covering his ass by accusing the only witness—me—of obstruction of justice.

I called Stacey from the car, and told her I was coming over. As I drove toward her office, with Stone following behind me in his Porsche, I hoped Elwood wouldn't try to make my life any more difficult than it already was.

NINETEEN

By the time I got to Stacey's office, I'd accepted that my day had not been perfect so far. Stone walked me from the car park to the lobby, and as we walked, I looked back over my shoulder, searching for an anonymous photographer.

The parking lot was half-empty, and the street behind us was semi-deserted. I didn't think anyone had tailed us on the drive here, but I couldn't see behind the car windows. Theoretically, someone might be sitting in one of the cars, watching me.

Stone escorted me up to the AAI reception, and then he said, "This is where I take off. Duty calls. I'll be at the casino tonight."

"You don't have to be."

He rolled his eyes. "You could just tell me when your shift ends. Hang on – aren't you having lunch with your parents today?"

"Ye-es," I said warily.

"Great. I'll join you then." I sighed and Stone said, "Hey, I like your mom's cooking."

I looked at him grimly, but I didn't say anything as he walked off.

Stacey's office seemed very quiet when I walked in, and it took me only a second to pin down the reason.

"Where's Sarah?" I asked her, and she sighed.

"At school."

"Oh, it must be nice to –" I was going to say 'have her out of your hair' but I stopped myself just in time and finished with, "work uninterrupted."

"It's not uninterrupted. I just got a call from Detective Elwood a few minutes ago, saying you might be trying to mislead the investigation."

I narrowed my eyes and clenched my jaw.

"Don't worry," Stacey told me, "the guy's clueless."

I breathed out and felt the tension leave my body. At least Stacey trusted me.

"Thanks," I said. "I came over to talk to you before handing over the report. I think we've got a suspect." Stacey raised one eyebrow silently, and I went on, "I think Jack Weber has something to do with this theft. His car's license plate is a partial match, and I think he looks a bit like the guy I saw jumping from the building."

"Hmm."

Stacey looked at me contemplatively, and I was a bit disappointed that she wasn't jumping up and down in excitement.

"What do you mean, 'hmm?'"

"Well…" She looked down and toyed with her pen, before continuing. "It's just a bit flimsy, seems a bit…forced." She looked at me again and said, "The guy's a big deal, a major player in the business community here. I don't think we should mess with him."

"So no-one's going to investigate him?"

"Oh, no, I'll ask someone to look into him. Discreetly, of course."

I nodded, not sure if I was pleased. "Do you want me to help out?"

Stacey shook her head. "It's not a priority. We're not likely to find anything on him, and short of finding the painting in his house – well, there's not much we can do about it."

"What about testing for DNA and fingerprints, that kind of stuff?"

Stacey gave me a funny look. "Hmm."

Realization dawned, and I almost said, "D'oh!" out loud. Of course – AAI wasn't interested in finding out who committed the crime, they were only interested in recovering the painting itself, so they wouldn't have to pay out the insurance premiums. For all I knew, they wouldn't even investigate Jack, especially now that they didn't have a PI on staff.

"Did you learn anything from Jeremy?" Stacey asked, and I shook my head.

"He didn't say much. I'll type up the report and email it to you."

"Thanks. We'll get in touch if we need any more work done."

We said our goodbyes, and I walked out feeling slightly dejected. Neither of the people I'd talked to about Jack had been interested in him, and I wondered if maybe I was wrong about him. That was impossible though – I had no doubt that the man I'd seen leaping from the building was Jack Weber. All I needed to do was to prove it, and then...

And then *what*, exactly? I hadn't been hired to look into the theft, and it wasn't any of my business. I'd stop caring about it, I told myself, and I'd stop wondering how Jack was involved.

———

As I DROVE away from the AAI office, I found myself checking over my shoulder, once in a while, wondering if anyone was following me. I felt safer in the stark daylight, and I was annoyed at myself for becoming so used to having Stone follow me around. I'm a PI. I need to take care of myself, even if it means learning to poke a guy's eyes out in self-defense. Stone was right – I needed to go back to my KravMaga lessons. By the time I walked into The Peacock Club, my mental resolve to take up KravMaga again was making me feel a lot better, even though I hate all the kicking and poking that it involved.

The Peacock Club is one of the more "boutique" strip clubs in Vegas, which means it's very slightly off-Strip, and has only a couple dozen exquisite-looking girls working there at a time, instead of a couple of hundred. The rates are also higher, and the clientele are mostly wealthy locals.

At this time of day, the club was practically empty. It wasn't very well-lit, with only a few strange, bluish lights glowing here and there, and when I stepped inside, I found myself blinking as I adjusted to the darkness. Bass thumped loudly from hidden speakers, and a lingerie-clad woman twirled around a pole on the big stage at the front of the room.

There was a bar along one wall, and the rest of the room was occupied by around fifty small, round tables. Darkly upholstered tub chairs surrounded each table, but only a few tables were occupied at this hour, mostly by single men chugging beers and glancing at the dancers on stage. Strippers hovered around them and every so often one of them would get up and follow a girl into one of the private lap-dance rooms.

I nodded to Greg, the DJ, and went over to say hello. We'd met during my last investigation, and he was a friendly guy who always seemed oblivious to the half-naked women around him. While Greg and I were catching up on our lives, Samantha popped up beside me. She was wearing white lace lingerie with silver high-heels, and she looked like something out of a Victoria's Secret catalogue. Maybe that's what I'd look like if I stopped eating so many cupcakes and bought myself some nice underwear.

"I saw you come in," she told me. "And I've got a ten minute break now. What's up?"

"I'd like to talk to some of Crystal's friends at the club," I said. "Do you know who they are?"

Samantha and Greg exchanged a glance.

"Crystal didn't have many friends here," Samantha said. "She liked to keep to herself."

Greg nodded. "Yeah. I'd talk to her once in a while, but I never saw her chatting with anyone else."

"Huh." I couldn't help being surprised. "Everyone on the movie set said she was friendly."

Samantha nodded. "She was, but she worried that the more people she made friends with here, the quicker her secret would get out. She was convinced she'd be a big Hollywood celebrity, and she didn't want anyone knowing she used to be a stripper."

I turned to Greg. "But she was friends with you?"

He grinned. "All the girls like me. How can you hate the only gay guy in a strip club?"

I smiled back. That explained how he was so oblivious to all the bare breasts surrounding him.

"What did you talk about?" I asked him.

"Just the usual. She'd get leads for parts, but usually they didn't work out. And then she got a serious lead for the part in Casino Kings, and she was real excited about that."

"Did she have any enemies? Anyone who might want to harm her?"

He shook his head. "She didn't try to make friends here, but that's normal. Lots of girls keep to themselves."

"Was she acting different before she died? Worried about anything?"

Greg frowned. "Not really. But she did mention that some guy was constantly bugging her and she wasn't interested. She said she'd have to deal with it."

I turned to Samantha. "Did she tell you anything about that?"

Samantha shrugged. "Guys come on to women like us all the time. We *do* work in a strip club. Crystal might've said something, but I don't remember."

"Was he someone she met here?" I asked Greg.

He shook his head, and sat quietly, trying to remember. "Some hotshot," he said finally. "I think he had something to do with Casino Kings."

I pulled out the list of names Tony had given me, and showed it to Greg. He read through the list and handed it back. "I'm sorry. I don't remember any names, but I think she said it was someone on the set."

Samantha looked somber. "I should've paid attention. I should've realized it was serious, not just some random creep."

"It's ok," I told her. "You had no way of knowing. Besides, we don't even know if this guy had anything to do with her death."

Samantha shook her head, and I knew that my words sounded hollow.

"Anyway," I said. "Do you know a Cheryl Czekanski?"

Greg and Samantha both made puzzled faces.

"A lot of girls here don't go by their real names," Samantha told me. "What's her stripper name?"

"I've got no idea. She might not even be a stripper."

"I know a Cheryl," Greg said. "See that red-head walking up to those two men? That's Cheryl Adams."

We all watched the red-head. She had a mass of long curls, and was wearing a tiny string bikini. Even from this distance, we could see the star tattooed on her lower back, and she glanced at us before sashaying off toward one of the private lap-dance rooms with a man following her.

We'd all looked away when Cheryl had glanced at us, looking obviously guilty.

"I don't think that's the Cheryl I'm after," I said, "But it's worth a shot."

"Why're you after Cheryl?" Samantha asked.

"Crystal made bank transfers to her…lots of money at a time. Do you know anything about that?"

Samantha shook her head. "Maybe it was someone in LA. Maybe a casting agent."

"Hmm," I said. "How long do these lap-dances last?"

"Longer than my break," Samantha said. "I'll be with you in a few minutes."

I watched as she walked away, swishing her hips as she approached a man sitting by himself in a booth. His face lit up immediately, and he stood up automatically and trotted after her like a dazed puppy.

I watched them disappear into a private room, feeling a bit awkward. Greg had his headphones on again, and was busy with his music. I noticed a bouncer glancing at me, and I didn't want to get kicked out for looking like a social worker, so I headed over to the bar, ordered myself a juice, and tried to chat with the sullen bartender.

My phone rang and I looked at the caller ID and sighed. I was tempted to let it just go on ringing, but that would just worry her even more. "Hi, Mom."

"Tiffany! Your Nanna just got a call from her friend Nancy who saw you walking into The Peacock Club."

"Yes, Mom. I'm just here to talk to someone."

She made a disapproving noise and said, "I don't want everyone to think my daughter's a stripper."

I rolled my eyes. Suburban moms are the same everywhere. "Maybe you shouldn't have named me 'Tiffany Black' then," I told her.

She made another disapproving noise and said, "When are you going to come over? It's almost lunch-time."

"Soon," I said, wondering if it was too late to make some excuse and not go. Free home-cooking was nice, but I didn't want Stone showing up with me at my parents' place again. I just knew they'd get the wrong idea. "But I'm a bit busy with work, maybe I could just—"

My mother interrupted me before I could finish. "Your nanna's invited some man over."

I groaned. "Nathan. I can't believe this."

"How do you know him?" my mom asked sharply. "Is he a friend of yours?"

I couldn't tell her that I'd met him during one of Nanna's poker games, so I muttered something about meeting him when I ran into Nanna and her friends at a buffet.

I didn't think I sounded convincing, but my mom seemed to buy the story. "How long ago was this?"

"Umm. Yesterday."

"Well. You should've told me."

"About what?"

"Your nanna says this man's her boyfriend, can you believe that? I want you to come meet him. Maybe she'll listen to you."

"Fine," I said. "I'll be there."

"Is Stone coming?"

She sounded hopeful and I frowned. A few weeks back she'd thought that we were dating, and no matter how often I told her we weren't, she kept hoping for a relationship between us. "No, he's not," I told her, sounding more annoyed than I'd meant to. Now I'd definitely have to talk him out of coming with me.

"Hmm," she said. "Don't worry. There are lots of men out there. Even if you broke up, you'll find someone new."

"We didn't break up. We were never together."

She started to say something about plenty of fish in the ocean but not enough time to waste and I let my head roll backwards. I couldn't take any more of her dating advice, so I said, "My appointment's here. Gotta go. I'll see you soon."

I hung up before she could tell me to keep my eyes open for a good man and to remember to wear nice clothes – there would be enough time for her to say all that during lunch.

———

SAMANTHA AND CHERYL came out of their rooms at about the same time. I exchanged a glance with Samantha and we went to talk to Cheryl.

"Hi, Cheryl," Samantha was saying when I reached her. "How's it going?"

"Not bad." Cheryl glanced at me with a questioning look.

I waited as Samantha introduced me and explained that I was looking into Crystal's death. As Samantha talked, I watched Cheryl's face.

Up close, I could tell that Cheryl was a little older than us, maybe in her late thirties. Her expression was guarded, and the angular contours of her face made her look slightly cynical.

I'd guess she was a parent, and that although she had a slim, supermodel-worthy figure and a face that looked stunning to me, she probably wasn't allocated the lucrative night shifts, the times when big spenders came out to play.

In a year or two she'd be older than all the other strippers here, and she'd probably have to leave The Peacock Club for one of the slightly less picky larger clubs. Or maybe by then she'd have accumulated a fortune and would retire to a beach in Costa Rica.

"I'm sorry about your friend," Cheryl told us when Samantha was done. "But I didn't know her, and I need to get back to work."

"Maybe we can chat during your break?" I asked her.

Cheryl's glance was slightly contemptuous. "I've got stuff to do during my break. And I don't want to be rude, but I didn't know Crystal, I never work weekends and according to you she only worked one weekend a month."

There was an undercurrent of resentment in her voice, and I knew my guess about her not getting the lucrative shifts was spot on.

"Come on, Cheryl," I said. "I think you know more than that."

Cheryl rolled her eyes. "I'm going back to work. Don't bother me."

She began to stalk off, trying to choose which of the men to talk to.

"Cheryl," Samantha called out after her.

A stripper wearing a "sexy nurse" outfit, sky-high red stilettos, and a vacuous expression turned around to look at us. She was wearing dark makeup, and her long blonde hair fell to her waist in big, loose curls. She looked familiar…

"Hang on," I said, rushing up to the blonde "nurse" before I'd sorted through my jumbled thoughts. "You're Cheryl. Cheryl Czekanski."

Samantha had followed me, and said, "No, her name's Sherry."

Sherry/Cheryl smiled at us. "Sherry's my stripper name," she said, and then lowered her voice to a breathy whisper. "My real name's Cheryl, but that's not quite as sexy." She giggled in a strange, high-pitched voice. "Do I know you?"

I smiled and shook my head, pleased with my hunch. She was one of the beautiful blondes my Google Images search had turned up, and she'd thought we were calling out to her earlier.

"I'm Tiffany Black," I told her. "I'm a private investigator looking in Crystal Macombe's death."

The smile disappeared from her face, and I knew I was onto something.

It was time to go on the offensive, so before she could think up a story, I said, "Why'd you kill her?"

Cheryl shook her head furiously. "I had nothing to do with her death." She moved to a quiet corner, away from the club patrons, and Samantha and I followed her.

We all stood huddled together, and Cheryl glanced from me to Samantha, who was standing there with her arms crossed, her face stony.

"That's a big claim," I said. "Especially when Crystal was sending you so much money each month."

"Why would I kill her?" Cheryl looked at me, all wide-eyed innocence. I half-expected her to flip her hair to make a point.

"What was the money for?" I asked.

Beside me, I could feel the anger emanating from Samantha. I turned to look at her, and flinched when I saw her narrowed eyes and pursed lips.

Cheryl stared at us wordlessly, her lips twisted into a sulky pout. Finally, she said, "I don't have time for this. I have to get back to work."

She took a step forward, and Samantha immediately moved to block her path. The two glared at each other, and I saw a bouncer glancing over at us nervously.

"Guys," I said, "I don't want either of you losing your jobs over this." I turned to Cheryl and said, "You don't *have* to talk to me – but if you really didn't have anything to do with Crystal's death, you should. Unless you *want* me to give the cops your details so you go to lockup for a few days. Your manager'll love that."

She glared at me and took a step back. "Fine," she hissed. "What d'ya wanna know?"

"Why was she sending you money?"

Cheryl glanced at Samantha again, and so did I. Samantha looked like she was ready to pounce at any moment now – her cheeks were flushed, and her hands were balled up into loose fists.

"Why don't you go back to work," I told Samantha. "I should talk to Cheryl in private."

Samantha shook her head. "No way. Bitch messed with my girl, maybe she killed her. I'd like to know."

I wanted to give Samantha a good shake, but I satisfied myself with grabbing her arm and dragging her a few steps backwards with me.

Cheryl stood in the corner, watching us with wary eyes.

"Look," I whispered, when we were out of earshot. "You need to let me do my job, ok? Maybe she knows something, but she won't tell me if you're there."

Samantha stared at Cheryl for a few seconds, and then sighed. "Fine. But you need to tell me what Airhead here says."

"Of course."

I watched Samantha sashay away, and then I went back to Cheryl and asked, "What happened between you and Crystal?"

Cheryl studied her perfect French manicure. "I wondered why Crystal only worked one weekend a month. I figured she either had another job or a sugar daddy. One time, I overheard her talking on the phone with some guy, telling him she loved him and she was at some modeling job and she missed him."

"So you blackmailed her."

Cheryl shrugged. "It wasn't really blackmail, if you think about it. I was doing her a favor."

"How?"

Cheryl looked at me blankly.

"How was it a favor?"

She shrugged again. "Fine. So it wasn't a favor. But I figured the bitch could pay me a bit of cash, it's not like she was hurting for it."

There was a pause as Cheryl frowned and studied a nail which seemed to be chipped.

I tapped one foot, trying not to be impatient. "Then what happened?"

She looked up at me. "Huh? Oh yeah, she stopped paying up. Told me to go eff myself, and I told her I would."

She frowned, remembering their fight, and I waited for a few seconds before prompting her. "And then?"

"I'm not as stupid as everyone here thinks," Cheryl said. "I took some photos of Crystal on my phone and then I mailed them to her boyfriend."

I listened to my heart thudding, wondering if I'd heard right. "You emailed her boyfriend?"

She shook her head. "No. I don't know his email. But I knew Crystal was staying at The P'lazzo, so I rang up and found their room number. Sent the photos by post."

"When was this?"

Cheryl tilted her head, thinking. "Couple of days back."

"And sending him the photos was meant to help, how?"

She looked at me steadily, not saying anything. I could almost see the wheels in her head turning slowly, trying to remember why she'd thought it'd be a good idea.

I sighed. "Did the boyfriend get in touch with you?"

"No. He didn't know I'd taken the photos."

I thought back to the conversation with Max. How sad he'd seemed, how proud that Crystal would get a part and that she had values and morals. That didn't seem like a man who'd found out that his girlfriend was a stripper. The guy must be one hell of an actor, I thought, not really wanting to believe it. Hopefully, he was still in Vegas.

"Thanks for your help," I told Cheryl, not really meaning it. "Don't leave town."

TWENTY

The drive to The Palazzo was short but nerve-wracking; I worried I wouldn't get to the hotel in time, and I drove like a woman possessed, trying to think of what to say if Max was still there.

I didn't bother to stop at the front desk, and went straight up and knocked on Max's suite. When he opened the door, I felt my body sag forward with relief.

"Max," I said, too happy to be worried anymore. "I'm glad you're here."

I walked in uninvited and sat myself down on the leather sofa. It was only then that I noticed Max looked different from the last time I'd seen him. His forehead was creased, and he seemed to be moving stiffly.

"How are you?" he asked mechanically, and I smiled, ready with my polite response.

He had his back to me, and I watched as he began to open a desk drawer.

I rose to my feet automatically. I was sure that Max was reaching for a gun and I fumbled for my bag, trying to undo the zip as quickly as possible.

Time slowed down. The room seemed really bright, and I couldn't hear any noise from outside. Why wasn't I carrying my gun today? I watched Max reach into the drawer and grab something, and there was my hand, inside my bag, wrapping around the bottle of pepper spray. Not that pepper spray would win a gunfight.

"My friend St—" I began, as Max turned around.

He wasn't holding a gun. There was a big white envelope in his hand, and I let my sentence hang in the air, unfinished.

"What about him?" Max said.

"Um, Stone, right," I babbled. Max didn't seem to want to kill me, but it might be a good idea to tell him the lie I'd just thought of. "He's waiting for me downstairs, we're meant to go somewhere after this."

My words didn't seem to register with Max – his eyes looked dull and lifeless. "I got this in the mail today."

He handed the envelope over to me, and I opened it and pulled out the photos of Crystal. They were low-resolution, blown up, and unflattering. There was Crystal dancing on a pole, and there she was leaning over some guy's table. There weren't any pictures of her actually giving a lap dance, but there were a few pictures of happy-looking men following a topless, flirta-tiously smiling Crystal. Looking at the pictures, I felt a little sick myself, and I could understand why Max was now sitting on the sofa, head in his hands.

"Why didn't she tell me?" he said. "If she needed money, I'd have been happy to pay. I guess she had her own sense of pride."

He looked up at me, his eyes silently pleading me to tell him something worth listening to.

"Uh," I said.

It's an act, I told myself, but I didn't believe that. Max looked so forlorn and dejected; I couldn't help but feel sorry for him.

"You know she was ambitious," I told him. "She probably wanted to earn her own money."

"But she could've told me. I could've gotten her a job as a secretary somewhere."

But then she wouldn't have been able to spend all her days chasing auditions. Being a weekend-stripper was a time-honored tradition among starlets, surely everyone in Hollywood knew that? But Max was just another clueless male.

"When did you get these?" I asked.

"A few minutes ago. I got a call from the front desk, so I went down, thinking it'd be business papers, but…"

I looked at the envelope. It was addressed to The Plassoo Casino, and I could imagine the postal workers scratching their heads over where it needed taking to.

I took a deep breath and sat down beside Max.

"Did you know about it?" he asked me, and I nodded.

"I'm sorry. I was told to keep it a secret."

"Does everybody know? Am I the last to find out? I really believed her, that she was doing modeling work. I feel like such an idiot."

"You're not an idiot. And nobody else knows, just me and Samantha. And I only know because Samantha told me."

He nodded unhappily, and I excused myself and headed down to the lobby. I needed a few minutes alone, and I needed to figure out how to validate or disprove what Max had just told me. I wandered down the hallway to the gift shops, where I watched the tourists poring over fancy dresses and over-priced watches. Cameras blinked, high up on the ceiling, and I knew that if I could just get into the surveillance room with its fancy monitors,

I could check the footage to see if Max had really gotten his mail today.

But that would involve calling in a favor from Stone, and I didn't want to do that. I found myself wandering back to the front desk, and the idea came to me.

Why hadn't I thought of this earlier? That's the problem with technology, I told myself, it makes you ignore real human beings. Oh no. That sounded like something Karma would say.

The man at the front desk was tall, thin and bespectacled. His name tag read "Geoff," and I went up to him and smiled.

He smiled back politely. "What can I do for you?"

"Did you just get an envelope addressed to The Plassoo Hotel?" I asked. "My friend just showed it to me and — was that for real?"

I half-frowned, half-smiled like I couldn't believe it, and Geoff chuckled. "Yeah. Just came in. Some people, huh?"

"Yeah," I said. "Some people."

I made my way slowly back to Max's room, thinking about his ignorance. But if he had nothing to do with Crystal's death, I was back to square one. Who could've possibly wanted Crystal to die?

TWENTY-ONE

I said goodbye to Max, and drove over to my parents' place, with Stone tailing behind me. I didn't have the heart to discourage Stone, and I was grateful for the company as he pulled up to the curb soon after me, and walked me to the door. We both glanced over our shoulders as we walked, but there were no other cars driving down the street, and no dangerous-looking photographer hovering nearby.

My mother opened the door, and looked slightly surprised to see Stone.

"It's lovely to see you," she said to him, and then turned me. "What a surprise."

I could see that she was slightly rattled, and Stone said, "I hope I'm not imposing. We should've called ahead."

"Oh, no," my mom said. "It's great to see you. I just didn't know you two were still together."

She looked at me suspiciously and I shook my head, "We're not. We were never together. We're just friends."

This was about the fiftieth time I've told my mother that, but she never seems to believe me. Stone and I followed her inside to the den, which was dark with its heavy drapes, and always ten degrees cooler than the temperature outside. When we got there, I saw why my mother had been so flustered to see Stone with me – there was another man sitting next to my dad. He looked about three feet wide, wore a checked shirt that he appeared to have slept in, and, judging from the strained look on my dad's face, seemed to have last showered a few months back.

Introductions were made all around, and it turned out that the obese man's name was Pearce. Nanna winked at me, and my mother said, "Stone's just a friend of Tiffany's. She's not dating anyone at the moment."

I rolled my eyes, and Pearce said, "How come you're still single? You look quite pretty."

"Thanks," I said. "How come you're still single?"

Pearce smiled broadly. "I've got very high standards."

I looked at Nanna, who made a face.

"So, what do you?" asked my dad.

"Video game reviews," said Pearce.

Stone frowned. "You upload videos of yourself playing video games?"

Pearce nodded. "Yep, but it's a bit more technical than that. You need to know Youtube and stuff."

"Doesn't sound technical to me," Nanna said. "I know how to use Youtube. I can do HTML and other coding, too."

Pearce looked at Nanna skeptically so I said, "She's right. She can do all that."

"So, what does it pay?" Nanna asked. "I bet it pays really well."

Pearce shrugged. "You've gotta hit it big."

"And have you?"

"I'm close."

"So it's not really making you any money," Nanna said.

"I make some."

"Enough to pay the bills?"

"I live with my parents, so I don't have to pay the bills."

"That must be fun," my dad said drily.

Stone looked at Pearce, one eyebrow raised one one-hundredth of an inch. Anyone else might think that Stone was just bored, but I knew from his mild expression that he was half-amused, half-disapproving.

Pearce didn't get my dad's sarcasm and shook his head. "No," he said regretfully. "They're always nagging me to vacuum and clean my room and stuff. I'm hoping to move out."

"Right," said my dad. "So you're looking for a job?"

"No," said Pearce. "I'm hoping to get a girlfriend. That way I don't have to pay the rent or vacuum or clean."

He smiled at me hopefully, and I said, "Don't look at me. I don't vacuum, clean or pay other people's rent."

The corner of Stone's mouth went up a tiny, near-invisible fraction of an inch. Pearce looked crestfallen and my mother said, "Tiffany. That's not very nice."

I shrugged. "At least I'm not a mooch."

"I can see why you don't have a boyfriend," Pearce said. "You aren't nice at all. I don't think you'll ever have a boyfriend."

"Yeah," I said. "But at least I've got a life."

Just then, there was a knock at the door, and my mother and I raced each other out to answer it. It was Nathan, standing there with a bunch of roses in his arms. I raised an eyebrow and my mother pursed her lips, but we didn't say anything about the flowers. Nathan followed us to the den, where he got the chance to give Nanna the flowers.

"I should've brought something," Pearce said, clearly unhappy at being upstaged, but unwilling to shell out the cash to actually bring something. I'd been expecting him to leave, but he seemed unwilling to miss out on a free lunch.

Nanna went to put the flowers away, and all of us turned our focus on Nathan. My dad and I wasted no time in quizzing him about his poker-playing, while Pearce just sat there sullenly, obviously hoping for lunch to be served soon. Stone leaned back in his chair and listened to Nathan, but didn't bother to ask anything.

"What're you doing while you're waiting to be a poker success?" I asked Nathan, just as Nanna returned to the room with the flowers in a big vase.

"I'm looking for work," Nathan said. "Maybe I'll be a valet. One of my friends is a valet, he said he'll set me up."

My father and I exchanged a glance. Valets in Vegas make more money than doctors in other cities, and I thought to myself that maybe Nathan wasn't a con artist after all. My mother said to him, "And you don't have a girlfriend?"

Nathan shook his head. "Haven't found the right woman."

"Tiffany's single," said my mother.

"I'm the one who invited Nathan over," said Nanna. "He's not interested in Tiffany."

Nathan smiled at Nanna and said, "That's true, I'm not. I prefer mature women. No offense," he added, turning to me.

Nanna and Nathan began to talk in low voices, and I couldn't hear what was being said, but after a few minutes, Nanna started to walk out of the room.

I looked at her questioningly, and she said, "I have to get something. "

With Nanna gone, my mother turned to Nathan again and said, "Are you sure you don't want to date someone a bit younger? Tiffany's pretty mature."

"Thank you," I said to her. "I am mature. But I don't want to date Nathan."

I smiled, pleased at having gotten to the rejection first.

"She's right," Nathan said. "I wouldn't want to date her."

"Besides," said Pearce. "That's why I'm here."

He leered at me, and I said, "Still not gonna pay your rent. Or do your vacuuming."

"If you want a boyfriend, you're gonna have to take care of him," Pearce said.

"Yeah," I said. "And he's gotta take care of me, too. And, you know, even take a shower once in a while."

"That's it!" Pearce said. "As soon as I've finished my lunch, I'm never gonna see you again."

I rolled my eyes. Why couldn't he be a man and leave, if he was so offended? I exchanged a glance with Stone, who was watching me through dark, amused eyes.

Nanna came back into the room carrying a thick book in her hand. "What'd I miss?" she said. "Why's everyone so quiet? Why's Pearce looking like a blowfish?"

"Tiffany's being rude to him," my mother said.

My dad turned to Pearce and said, "Why don't I pack you some lunch? That way you don't have to listen to Tiffany's rudeness. You can just take the lunch with you and leave."

"That'd be great!" said Pearce, still oblivious to sarcasm.

I shot Dad a grateful look, and my mother stood up. I heard the steel in her voice as she said, "Come on, Pearce, I'll pack you some lunch."

She stalked into the kitchen, and Pearce waddled after her happily.

"What's that book in your hands?" my dad asked Nanna.

She held it up and we all read the title: *Texas Hold 'Em Poker Probabilities: Strategies for Winning*. It was a hardcover book, two inches thick, and it didn't look like a fun read.

"It's for Nathan to borrow," Nanna said. "He's trying to improve his game."

"Yes," my dad said. "But why do *you* have it?"

Nanna and I stared at each other for a split second, and then I glanced at Nathan, who was clearly in on the secret as well. My parents wouldn't approve if they found out Nanna's a regular at the poker tables, so that's information we've chosen to keep from them.

"Uh," Nanna hesitated. "It belongs to Tiffany."

"Yeah," I said. "I was just carrying it around with me."

My dad gave me a look, like he didn't quite believe me, but before he could say anything else, my mother stomped back into the room.

"He's gone now," she told me. "Happy?"

"I am, actually," I said. "I can't believe you wanted to set me up with him."

She gave me a despairing look, and then caught a glimpse of the poker book.

"What's that?" she asked, and Nanna said, "It belongs to Tiffany. Nathan's going to borrow it."

"Sure," my mother said, clearly not interested in poker books. Nanna's secret was safe for now, and my mother turned to me again. "Why can't you just be polite, for once? How am I ever going to have grandkids if you keep driving men away?"

"He was a leech," I said, "Not a man."

We headed over to the dining room and I suffered through an awkward lunch. Nathan got a phone call in the middle of lunch, and he said it was his valet friend wanting to introduce him to his manager, so he left before dessert.

None of us were sure what Nathan was doing with Nanna – except for Nanna, of course, who said he was interested in her romantically. Because of her charm, wit and beauty. All of us, except for Stone, rolled our eyes.

As soon as I'd finished my dessert, I headed into my parents' guest room and gave Minnie, Crystal's friend from the movie set, a call.

TWENTY-TWO

"**D**id you know anything about Crystal fending off unwanted advances?" I asked her. "She told a friend something about that. Said it was someone from the set."

Minnie thought for a moment and said, "One of the producers, Ben McAllister. He's got a roving eye, likes to give the girls a private screen test before he signs them on."

"You think it was him?"

"I'm not sure. She never mentioned nothing to me, it could've been anyone."

"What about the other producer? Jack Weber?"

"Yeah, I know he exists."

"Ever seen him?"

"No, he never comes on set. Lets Sam do whatever."

I thanked her and hung up, and then I dialed Ben McAllister's number, hoping I could score an appointment with him immediately.

"I'm investigating Crystal Macombe's death," I told him when he answered. Impersonating a federal officer is a crime, so I wasn't quite *impersonating*, just being a bit vague about the fact that I was a private investigator.

Ben listened to me politely and said, "I'm in LA at the moment, but I'll be back in Vegas on Saturday. Why don't we chat then?"

I agreed reluctantly, not sure what else I could do. Theoretically, I could ask Samantha to pay me to go up to LA, but I wanted to put that off, if possible. Besides, it was just one extra day.

When I got back to the den, I found my parents interrogating Nanna about Nathan.

"Something's wrong with him," my dad was saying, and my mother agreed.

"What do you think?" Nanna asked Stone, and everyone turned to him.

He looked back at us seriously. "You really want to know?"

There was a chorus of yeses from my parents and Nanna, and then he said, "I think he wants some advice. Someone friendly to teach him how to get by in Vegas and play poker." He turned to Nanna and added, "You're probably the nicest and most helpful person he met here."

Everyone looked serious, and I could see my mother feeling sorry for the poor young kid who was new to this town. She'd probably be inviting him over for another lunch soon.

"Well, I should go," I announced. "I've got an early shift today."

"Nathan left his book behind," my mother told me. "You should take it back with you."

I glanced at Nanna, and she nodded too, so I picked up the heavy book, and took it with me. I wasn't sure what I'd do with it, but I didn't seem to have much choice.

I RARELY DID afternoon shifts at The Treasury — and every time I did, I wished I could do more of them. The crowd was thinner after lunch; the tourists either eating, shopping, or sleeping off their previous long night. The gamblers were mostly tired from staying up the night before, and they didn't usually have the energy to be angry about anything. They played mechanically, and I smiled and made polite chit-chat just as mechanically.

It was only eight-thirty when my shift ended, and I checked my phone to find that Nanna had sent me a text: "Stp b t borgata wk u hm."

I rolled my eyes and wondered just how Nanna had learnt to text, and why she had her autocorrect switched off. Or maybe it was switched on and worked with a convoluted, Nanna-like logic. Most of the letters made no sense to me, but The Borgata Casino was on my way home, and I figured I'd stop by. If Nanna wasn't there, I'd call her.

Stone was waiting for me in the lobby and he joined me as I strolled down the Strip.

"You don't have to do this," I told him, but he just looked at me cynically and said nothing.

"This feels ridiculous," I said after a while.

Still nothing.

He plopped himself down on a sofa in The Borgata lounge and pulled out his smartphone, while I went to look for Nanna. Sure enough, she was at one of the poker tables, playing a hand intently. I watched her win the hand, and then she looked up and noticed me.

"That's my grand-daughter," she told the table as she left.

"Good night?" I asked her when she joined me.

"The best. The tourists are just coming in for their long weekend, and they're all fresh and reckless."

"So why'd you text?"

Nanna gave me a funny look. "You need to learn to read texts, Tiff. It's what all the cool kids are doing these days. Much faster than writing."

"Yes, but what does it *mean?*"

"I'll walk you home," she said. "Unless you have that 'Winning Poker Formulas' book on you now?"

I shook my head, and we headed for the exit. Stone joined us and Nanna said, "I'm not interrupting anything, am I?"

I sighed and shook my head. "Stone was just leaving."

I looked at him pointedly, but he kept walking with us.

"Doesn't look like he's leaving," Nanna said, and I gave Stone another stern look.

"Just ignore me," he told Nanna.

"Well," she said. "Maybe I'm the one who should head home. Leave you two alone."

I groaned. "It's not what you think. Stone, you can leave us here, Nanna can walk me up."

He looked from me to Nanna and said, "You've got to be on your own at some point, and I suppose Nanna can take care of you."

"I sure can," she said drily, and Stone left without another word.

"Maybe I should've left," Nanna mused, as we walked to my condo. "Maybe you two could've had something."

"No," I said. "We're not 'having' anything."

She kept bugging me about Stone all the way to my front door. I tried to convince her that Stone was just walking me home to keep me safe, but I was distracted by our conversation and when I opened my front door, it took me a few seconds to register what I was seeing.

There was no envelope lying on the middle of the floor today. Instead, there was a big, white piece of poster paper, lying in the middle of my living area, the word "SURPRISE" written on it in red crayon.

"Crayon," Nanna said from behind me. "Whoever writes with crayon these days?"

"Stay here," I told her, trying to keep calm.

I was straining my ears, trying to hear something. Every tiny noise seemed to jump out at me, and I was convinced that someone else was in the condo with us. Were the curtains rustling? Was that someone breathing? I took a tentative step toward my bedroom door. My hands were cold and clammy and I reminded myself to stay calm.

I took a deep breath and was about to take another step, when Mr. Beard stepped out of the bedroom and into the living area.

"Surprise!" he said softly. "Are you surprised to see me?"

My eyes widened and my heart seemed to have stopped beating altogether. Despite it failing to pump blood around my body, I managed to take a slow step back, and asked, "What're you doing here?"

The last time I'd seen him was in the backroom of The Riverbelle Casino, after I'd driven my stiletto heel into his neck. I knew he'd been arrested as part of the casino fraud ring, and I'd expected him to be waiting out his days behind bars.

He looked just the same as he had the last time I'd seen him – wide and muscular, with his thick body stuffed into dirty jeans and a faded grey t-shirt. He was bald, and was clean-shaven other than his close-clipped French beard.

He smiled, a wide, maniacal smile. "Stupid bitch. Didn't you understand the photos? I'm here to kill you, see?" He lifted his right hand high into the air, and I saw he was carrying a big knife, its blade glinting in the light.

I took another step back, and heard Nanna say, "That's an expensive-looking knife. You sure you wanna get blood on it? A gun seems more practical."

Mr. Beard said, "Yeah, right? I'd like to use a gun, but this about getting even." His eyes glistened and he said to me, "I've still got that scar on my neck. I reckon I should give *you* one."

He lunged at me and I screamed and turned around.

"Run!" I told Nanna, but she was already ten steps ahead of me. She'd probably crept out after giving Mr. Beard that idea about shooting me.

I caught up with her and grabbed her wrist. A door was cracked open in front of us – some nosy neighbor must've been trying to eavesdrop on us, and I pushed Nanna inside, and locked the door behind us.

"Hey!" A plump man with curly orange hair glared at us. "This is *my* apartment!"

"Yeah," Nanna said. "But you were listening to *our* private conversation!"

There was a loud banging at the door, and we all froze.

"Open up!" Mr. Beard yelled. "I know you're in there."

There was the sound of a door creaking open, and I heard a familiar shuffling.

"What's all this ruckus?" Mrs. Weebly's voice rang out, and then the shuffling stopped and I heard a high-pitched scream, followed by footsteps and a slammed door.

"I'm calling the police!" Mrs. Weebly yelled through her door. "You better be gone! We don't tolerate that kind of thing, here."

I heard a growl from the other side of the door, and then Mr. Beard said in a soft, sing-song voice, "Tee-fanny. I know you're in there. And you know I'll be back."

There was a sharp thud, and then I heard footsteps walking away. I peered out through the fisheye and saw nothing.

My heart was thumping loudly and I breathed in deeply. I could breathe again, I realized. That was a good thing.

The orange-haired man said, "Wow. That guy seems nasty."

"He's terrible," Nanna agreed. "What kind of man wants to stab my grand-daughter?"

I turned around and frowned at her. "What's with telling him to shoot me?"

"I was trying to reason with him," Nanna said. "I thought he'd change his mind, and go looking for a gun."

"The guy's nuts," I said. "You can't reason with a guy who's nuts."

"Good point."

I opened the door a crack and peered out. "Nobody there," I called.

And then I opened the door and saw the knife stuck to it.

"Oh, shit," the orange-haired man said.

Nanna crossed her arms and pursed her lips disapprovingly. "He ruined that knife anyway."

"Sorry about your door," I told the orange-haired guy. "Hang on."

I grabbed the knife and pulled, but it wouldn't come out.

"I'll do it," he said.

He grabbed the knife and pulled, but it refused to budge.

"I wasn't really trying," he told us, and then he tried again.

He continued to pull at the knife for a good five minutes. There was some grunting, some swearing, and then finally the knife budged a bit.

"I'm sorry about the door," I told him again. "I can ask my friend to come fix it."

"No, it's fine," he said. "I'm Ian, by the way. Ian Ewanson."

"That's a tough name," Nanna told him. "Your parents must love tongue-twisters."

Ian smiled. "No, but they sure can pick a name."

I looked around the condo. The man looked like he was in his mid-thirties, but the place seemed to belong to a teenager. There was a Star Wars poster on the wall, and a wall of collected science-fiction toys. There were three bean bags, a couch that looked like it'd been picked up off the curb, and a dirty shag rug.

Nanna was introducing us, and I waved at Ian distractedly as he continued to struggle with the knife.

"You live here by yourself?" I asked, and he nodded, pulling the knife out with one final grunt.

"Got it," he said, and held it above his head like a trophy.

I flinched. "Maybe you could put it down?"

"Oh, right." He carried it over to his shelf of action-figures and put it beside one. "This is pretty exciting, it's the coolest thing that's happened here all week. You must have a really fun life."

"Sure," I said. "It's pretty fun when there aren't any maniacs trying to kill me."

"That's the best part," Ian said. "The way you screamed and ran away, that was awesome." I pursed my lips and he added, "Of course, if you hadn't escaped, I'd have gone in and saved you."

I raised an eyebrow. "Would you? You seemed pretty annoyed when we barged into your place."

"Yeah," he said. "But that was before I knew you were this cool private eye."

"That's nice of you to offer to save us," Nanna told him. "You don't meet young men who are so chivalrous, these days." She turned to me and said, "Isn't he a nice young man, Tiffany?"

Ian beamed and asked me, "How come you didn't just shoot the guy? Detectives in all the movies I've seen just whip out their guns and shoot."

"I wasn't carrying a gun."

He frowned. "Why not?"

"Yeah," Nanna said. "Why not?"

I felt my left eye begin to twitch. "Because I have to go in and out of casino security all the time," I told them. "You can't take a gun into a casino."

They nodded, and Ian said, "What about Kung-Fu? Don't you know Kung-Fu?"

I stared at him and he said, "I guess not. Figures. You don't look like you can do Jackie Chan kicks."

He looked slightly disappointed and I scowled. "I don't want to beat up a guy in the hallway," I told him. "Detectives and cops sometimes don't get along."

He brightened up. "You know what you need? You need a bodyguard."

"Right." As though I hadn't just been wondering whether or not to swallow my pride and tell Stone that I'd like him to follow me around all day.

"Hey!" he said, struck by a brainwave. "How 'bout I be your bodyguard?"

"Isn't that a lovely idea!" Nanna said. "That would be good for you."

"Umm, I don't think so," I said. "Besides, don't you have to go to work or something?"

159

He shook his head. "Nah, I just live off my trust fund. I've been looking for something cool to do. Maybe I could be your partner?"

He looked at me hopefully and I said, "No. I do my own detecting."

"Oh, ok. I just thought I might help out." He looked crestfallen, and Nanna gave me a Look.

I sighed, wondering why I felt guilty. "Do you have any bodyguard experience?" I asked.

Ian smiled. "Sure. I go to the gym every day –" Probably to sit around the salad bar, eating pasta and cake, I thought. "– And I used to walk my sisters home from school when we were younger."

My phone buzzed with a text, and I looked down. It was Stone, checking that I'd got home ok.

"Besides," Ian was saying. "I'm looking to invest some money. Maybe I could buy a share in your detective company."

I looked at him steadily. Money would be nice. Money would mean I could leave my job at the casino and not have to stress about bills. Money would mean an actual office, so clients could find me, and maybe a website, and maybe…

Snap out of it, I told myself. The guy was a flake. One moment he'd be financing my business, the next moment he'd be dressing up like Superman. I couldn't deal with him. On the other hand, a bodyguard who wasn't Stone might be a nice change.

"I'll think about it," I told him, and Nanna and I left.

But not before Ian handed me his card, and told me he'd get us cool business cards for "our" private investigations firm.

TWENTY-THREE

I'd changed into my jammies and was contemplating brushing my teeth, when there was a knock at the door. I peered out carefully, half-expecting to see Mr. Beard or some other goon he'd hired, but it was just Ian.

I opened the door.

"I was thinking," he told me. "This building isn't very safe for private investigators. There's no security downstairs, and anyone could just climb up the fire escape and get in through the veranda. And the doors are flimsy, and –"

"Ian. I'm trying to get some sleep."

He blinked and seemed to notice my jammies for the first time. "Oh. Right. Well. I'll talk to you tomorrow, then."

I sighed and shut the door behind him, and decided I deserved a piece of chocolate or a cupcake after that conversation. There were a few cupcakes left in the box Glenn had given me yesterday, and I was saving them for tomorrow's breakfast, but maybe I should just have them now. I stared at the closed box, trying to decide if I should just go ahead, when there was another knock on my door.

I went over, peered through the fisheye, and opened it again for Ian.

"I know you said you were going to sleep," he said. "But don't you think it's too dangerous to sleep here? You know, that guy could just break in when you're sleeping. He'd just put a pillow over your head and you wouldn't even notice."

"He wants to stab my neck," I said icily.

"Yeah, well. Same thing. He could just slip in through the window quietly–"

"Ian. I need to sleep."

"Right. Right. Well, we'll talk tomorrow."

I closed the door as he left and leaned my forehead against it. Probably better to have the cupcakes now, I thought. And come to think of it, maybe I should just stay up all night so Mr. Beard couldn't stab me in my sleep.

There was another knock, and I opened the door and glared at Ian. "What?"

"Um, I was just thinking. Now that I'm going to be a private investigator and all…Are there any books I should read? Any websites that teach you all the cool tricks? You know, I want to get a headstart on learning all this pr– "

I tried to keep my voice steady. "Ian. Go. To sleep." I slammed the door shut in his face.

I heard Ian shuffle away back to his condo, and I groaned. He'd be back within ten minutes, max. Even without the threat of Mr. Beard breaking in and killing me in my sleep, there was no way I'd get any sleep here tonight.

I changed, packed an overnight bag and stepped out of my condo. I was locking my door when Ian came up. I stifled my sigh.

"Where are you going?" he said. "Do you have a safe house? Are you staying at your boyfriend's place?" He walked with me to the elevator. "It's a good thing you're leaving. It's probably good to lay low, once in a while."

He stepped into the elevator with me, and I wondered if I could choke him now while no-one was watching.

"Where are you going?" he asked.

"Checking into a casino."

"That's cool. Maybe I should check in, too."

"No!" I said quickly. "You should stay here, keep an eye out in case Mr. Beard returns."

Ian tapped his temple. "Good thinking. That's why you're the lead detective. I can be the brawn."

Ian was more fat that brawn, but I kept that thought to myself as I stepped out into the foyer.

"Are you walking to the casino?" Ian said. "I should escort you."

I was about to say no, but I paused. Driving up the Strip at this hour was an impossibility, given the number of tourists stopping to take photos of the lights. And walking by myself did seem a bit worrisome. If Ian was with me, I probably wouldn't have to check over my shoulder every two seconds.

"Ok," I said.

"Really?" His eyes shone and I was surprised he wasn't jumping up and down in delight. "That's great! This is my first case!" We'd reached the street by now, and Ian was walking beside me, looking from side to side every other second. "I'll do a really good job protecting you, I promise. I've got a yellow belt in karate."

"From when you were five?"

"Twelve, actually."

"Oh."

"I'd offer to carry your bag, but I've got to keep my hands free to beat up anyone who threatens you."

"That's fine," I told him. "My bag's pretty light."

I had the day off work tomorrow, so I didn't have to check into The Treasury, or any place within walking distance. But the last time I'd checked into a casino because I was scared for my life, it had been The Tremonte. I knew it was safe, they had a great breakfast buffet, and ok – maybe a little part of me was hoping that Jack would be there.

We trudged down the street, and Ian said, "This is really exciting for me, you know. All my life, I've been trying to find the right thing to do. You know, your career should be something you love, not just something that makes you money."

"You're right," I said. "But it's a little harder when you actually need money."

Ian shook his head. "Money is both a blessing and a curse," he intoned, and I gave him a funny look. "Sometimes I wonder how things would've been if I hadn't invested in that start-up. I might've finished college, maybe gotten a proper job."

"Hang on, I thought you had a trust fund."

"Yeah," he said. "I sold out my share of the company, and my parents made me put it all in a trust fund, and now I need to get my financial advisor's approval to spend more than a certain amount."

"So, you're telling me you founded a startup?"

He shook his head. "Oh no, I just invested a couple of grand in this thing some friends started. And then it got big and did an IPO and I cashed out. And then afterwards the stock tanked."

He had a guilty look on his face, kind of like a puppy who'd been bad.

"It wasn't your fault," I told him.

"Yeah, but other investors lost money on the stock. It was the dot-com bubble, except we didn't know it, back then."

We walked a few more paces and then he said, "But I'm happier with the money, of course. It's not that much, but I can survive without a job, and now I can pursue my true passion."

"Which is…?"

"I'm not sure." We'd reached the Strip by now, and stopped to stare as a limo full of shrieking girls drove past us. "At first I thought I might be an actor. But then I didn't get any work, and I realized I can sing and play the guitar, so I started a band. But nobody took me seriously with my orange hair, so I shaved it all off. And then people started wanting me to join their Neo-Nazi groups, so I got a big black wig. But then my parents didn't let me wear the wig when I went to visit them, and besides, it was itchy, so I got rid of it and grew my hair out."

We were almost at The Tremonte when another limo drove past us. There were three girls standing up through the sunroof, whooping like crazy people, and one of them pulled up her top and flashed her boobs at us.

Ian froze and stared at her until the limo drove out of sight. "Wow," he said, once it was gone and he got his voice back. "I love Vegas."

I looked at him and rolled my eyes. He'd be terrible bodyguard – a girl could parade topless in front of him, and he wouldn't even notice if I was bludgeoned to death right next to him. Still, it was a bit comforting to have him around. Now I could understand why people get themselves a small, friendly dog and claim it's good for security.

"So," I said. "You moved to Vegas for the girls, huh?"

"No, no." Ian shook his head. "I thought I'd play professional poker. But then I lost some money – practice money, right? But my financial advisor wouldn't let me take out more funds, so…"

"Your advisor sounds like a tightass."

Ian tilted his head slightly. "I guess he is. But John's just looking out for me. One time, I tried to get married, and he found out that the girl had married some poor loser before me and taken half his cash in the divorce. And then when I showed her a pre-nup she broke it off."

I looked at him to see if seemed heartbroken, but he was pretty stoic about it. "When was this?" I asked.

"Last week."

"Oh."

"Yeah, that's why I'm so excited to be a private eye now. It'll give me something to do."

We walked into The Tremonte, and the air conditioning hit me like a bucket of cold water. I breathed in deeply, letting my body get used to the chill.

"This is a cool place," Ian told me. "They've got a pretty good breakfast buffet. Maybe I should check in, too."

"No," I told him. "Remember you're meant to look out for Mr. Beard?"

"Oh, right."

We walked up to the front desk, and I asked for a standard room.

"You should let me pay," Ian said, fishing out his credit card. It gleamed dark black in the light, and he handed it over to the receptionist.

"No," I said quickly. "We're not partners yet."

The receptionist looked at me questioningly, and I shook my head at her, and gave her my plain low-rate card.

"That's ok," Ian was saying. "I don't mind paying."

"You shouldn't let people take advantage of you." The girl who didn't sign the pre-nup flashed into my head, and I was outraged on Ian's behalf.

"I don't mind paying sometimes," Ian said. "Or all the time."

I signed the hotel paperwork, and told Ian to be careful on the walk back to the condo. I wasn't really concerned about

Mr. Beard or some mugger attacking him. I was more worried that some topless girl would charm the pants off him and go home with his black card.

———

I DUMPED MY bag on the floor of the room, and stood by the window, fantasizing about the big buffet breakfast I'd eat tomorrow morning, when the in-room phone rang.

It wasn't a noise I'd been expecting, so I stared at the phone suspiciously, half-expecting that the noise had come from the room next to mine. But it rang once again, so I walked over and peered down at the display, which said "Reception."

I breathed a sigh of relief. I hadn't even known I'd been holding my breath, but now that I knew the call was from Reception, I didn't have to worry about Ian being in an emergency. I answered, hoping that it wasn't Ian calling from Reception to remind me about something inane.

"Please hold," the male voice told me, and I wondered if I'd won some kind of sweepstakes just by checking in, and maybe I'd get free home delivery of a dozen cupcakes each week.

My food lust returned with a vengeance, and I was lost in a mental debate between chocolate cupcakes vs vanilla, when a voice at the other end said, "Hi Tiffany. This is Jack Weber."

It was clear that I hadn't won my cupcake sweepstakes, so I wasn't as excited as I would've been normally. Still, my heart did a little flip, and I barely managed to stammer out a response.

"I saw you check in," he said. "Is everything ok?"

I didn't know who Jack really was, and I didn't really know whether he was an art thief or not. So of course, there was no reason for me to hope that there would be anything between us at all. No reason, other than a tiny cavewoman part of my brain which hoped that Jack wasn't calling for professional reasons.

And that cavewoman part of me knew that a guy might get turned off if I said, "A maniacal thug's trying to kill me, so I'm just hiding out here."

The cavewoman part prompted me to stammer a lot and say, "Uh. Um. Yeah. Uh. My condo. It's being repainted. Um."

"Oh, ok. Was that your boyfriend dropping you off?"

"Boyfriend?" I frowned and took a moment to process the word. No, the only person who'd been with me when I checked in was…Oh, right. "That was my neighbor."

"Seeing you off safely?"

"Something like that." I wondered if I detected a note of jealousy in his voice. Or maybe that was just wishful thinking.

"I'm calling because I'm about to take a break from work," Jack said. "And I wondered if you'd like to come and talk about Casino Kings and Crystal?"

I glanced at the bed with regret. An early night, followed by an early and massive breakfast had been my plan, but it was almost ten and what was another hour?

"Sure," I said. "Are you taking your break now?"

As soon as I said the words I frowned. The man claimed he was bored of business, but if he was at work so late at night, he had to be a workaholic – or maybe he just started his day late. Or maybe he was a vampire.

Either way, we decided to meet in ten minutes at the café opposite the blackjack tables. I hung up, went to the bathroom and changed into a prettier top, realized he must've seen

168

me walk in wearing a different top via the security cameras, changed back into my original clothes, and decided to pile on some mascara and lipstick instead.

———

I TRIED TO time my entrance carefully. I didn't want to come to the café too early and look like a desperate loser, but I also didn't want to be too late.

I used the extra minute I had before our meeting to call Emily. I got her voicemail, and left a message telling her that it was Mr. Beard who'd been threatening me. Oh, and yeah, he'd tried to kill me.

I hung up and headed down to the café, worried that I was still going to be early. Thankfully, when I got there, Jack was leaning back in an armchair opposite a low table, nursing a dark-looking drink in a white mug and reading something on his phone. He'd clearly come straight from his office – which I assumed was upstairs – and was wearing a perfectly-cut, dark gray suit, and a white shirt with no tie. Silver cufflinks peeked out from beneath his suit sleeves. He looked like something out of a glamorous movie, and a shiver of excitement ran down my spine before I could stop it. The man's probably a criminal, I reminded myself, and he doesn't seem quite normal.

Jack looked up as I approached, his eyes glinting emerald in the dim café lighting, and I felt my heart thud loudly, my mental warnings forgotten.

"You're here," he said, smiling as I settled myself into the chair opposite him. "I was just about to order myself a cupcake. Would you like one, too?"

I stared at him in disbelief. How had he read my mind? But I was too nervous to trust myself around food now. I'd be unable to swallow a single bite, and I'd waste a whole cupcake. The guilt of that wasted cupcake would gnaw at me every day for the rest of my life.

I shook my head, no and he waved a fawning waitress over. We placed our coffee orders, and Jack asked for a triple-chocolate cupcake as well. I tried to ignore my pang of regret.

Our proximity was making my heart beat erratically, and I worried that pretty soon I'd start acting like a teenager with a silly crush. I wanted to seem professional. Calm and composed, not nervous or flustered, so I jumped straight into work.

"This is a list of people who're working on Casino Kings," I said, showing Jack the list the cameraman, Tony, had given me.

He ran his eyes down and nodded. "I don't know most of them," he said. "But I'll try to answer your questions."

"Well, your co-producer, Ben. Do you know him?"

Jack leaned back and looked at me carefully. "I do," he said carefully. "He's an interesting guy."

"How so?"

Jack shrugged. "He's always busy, loves showbiz. Some people think he's a bit rude, and at times he drinks too much. He likes women. Maybe more than he should."

I frowned at that last bit. "Crystal claimed that someone on the movie set was pestering her with unwanted advances."

I felt a smidgen of stress that the someone might be Jack. But that wasn't possible, I told myself – according to Minnie, Jack never went on set and he hadn't even known Crystal.

Our coffees arrived and Jack looked at his cupcake. "Are you sure you don't want something to eat?"

I shook my head resolutely. "I've heard other people say that Ben liked his women. That he'd only sign them onto a movie after they'd paid him a few private visits."

Jack's eyes were guarded. "I don't want to get Ben in trouble. But the rumors were pretty spot on. He's a nice enough guy, though."

"Other than forcing women to sleep with him."

"These girls think that sleeping with a producer's going to help their careers. I'm not defending what he does, but his attitude is that it's a give and take. Nobody forces anyone."

It was a morally ambiguous area and I made a face. Living in Vegas, you see a lot of "give and take" like that, and I let the topic slide. Instead, I said, "Do you know where he is, now?"

Jack shrugged. "Probably in LA. He's usually there during the week. He's got business in Vegas, but when he comes here he usually stays at his cousin's place, not that hotel address that's written on your list."

"What cousin's place?"

"I don't have the address on me. But it's up north, just past Aliente."

The world went still for a moment. "Crystal's body was found up north. Just past Aliente."

I stared into my coffee, trying to make sense of it. It could just be a coincidence, but in my experience, coincidences don't happen very often. There were a number of reasons why Crystal might've gone up near where Ben was staying, and I didn't want to jump to conclusions.

"Ben's coming into Vegas on Saturday," Jack was saying. "I guess you'll go talk to him then?"

I nodded, still thinking about Crystal's death.

Jack said, "How's the Van Gogh investigation going?"

The question made me blink and stare at him carefully. Jack's face was a study in polite interest, but I caught a glimmer of amusement in his eyes, as well as a hint of genuine curiosity.

"Not bad," I said, unwilling to admit that I wasn't really investigating it. "Do you have any idea what might've happened?"

Jack smiled, and I watched his eyes. They gave nothing away and he said lightly, "Jeremy tells me that someone switched off the central security circuit, picked the lock on his door, and took off with the painting."

"How?"

Jack shrugged. "Who knows? But a window in Jeremy's apartment was found wide open. Maybe the guy jumped out of it."

The polite smile never left his face and we stared at each other, neither willing to be the first to look away.

I took a sip of my coffee and said, "Do you like extreme sports?"

I saw him look surprised for the first time since I'd sat down. "How d'you mean?"

I waved my hands dramatically. "Games. That are thrilling. And exciting." He looked amused by my theatrics, so I said, "You mentioned being bored by your work. I figured you might do something exciting to relieve the boredom."

Jack leaned forward. "In that case, yes. I do like excitement sometimes. Would you like to try something exciting with me?"

I paused for a split second, unable to help my mind from straying. And then I managed to say, "Being a private investigator is pretty exciting."

"Sure." He leaned back and we watched each other carefully.

"Do you like art?" I asked.

Jack nodded. "Who doesn't? Whoever stole that Van Gogh must've had great taste."

Ah-ha! "How do you know which painting was stolen?"

Jack smiled. "Jeremy showed me the painting when he had me over for a dinner party. When it was still hanging there, of course."

"Oh." My disappointment must've showed, but I ignored it and said, "So you're a Van Gogh fan?"

"I love his work. What do you think?"

Before I could answer, my phone rang. Emily.

I excused myself and went off into the lobby to talk about Mr. Beard and maniacs.

"What's his real name?" Emily asked me. "We know he's got a record, but I can't ask anyone to be on the lookout if I don't have his name. There were about a dozen guys arrested in that casino fraud ring."

I thought back. "Sorry. I've always thought of him as Mr. Beard. Even when he was arrested, I never bothered to find out his real name."

"Hmm."

I felt a prickle of worry. "Is that a problem?"

"We'll have to figure out what his name is. Maybe he left some DNA at your place?"

"He was carrying a knife – Ian's got it."

"Who's Ian?"

"Oh, he's this really nice neighbor of mine. He'll give you the knife."

I gave her Ian's number, and we hung up, but not before I asked her what she was doing up so late.

"Working," she said with a sigh. "No wonder I'm still single."

I agreed. "It's these Vegas hours. Decent men…" I trailed off, as soon as I realized I was starting to sound like Mrs. Weebly.

173

I headed back to the café and Jack and I chatted a bit more about art and post-impressionism, and then I stood up to go back to my room.

"Why don't I give you a free upgrade," Jack said. "I own most of this place, after all. And I happen to know that the Presidential Suite is empty tonight."

I stared at him. "Why would you do that?"

The words "you just met me," and "I'm not going to sleep with you," seemed to hang in the air. I wasn't sure I meant that second one, but it would be a good thing if Jack believed it.

"I like you," Jack said. "And if you don't like presidential suites, I can always give you a honeymoon suite."

I leaned back, narrowed my eyes and tilted my head. "Is this a bribe?"

Jack smiled and mock-raised his hands. "Whoa. Where's that coming from?"

"I know you're involved in the Van Gogh theft. I know you don't want me to look into it." Inspiration hit. "And I know you bribed the other investigator to get her off the case."

The smile left Jack's face and he squared his shoulders.

"Fine," he said. His voice was light, but he crossed his arms. "If that's what you think, you can stay in that crappy room you booked into."

"It's your casino. If the room's crappy, that's your fault."

He smiled, his eyes twinkling with amusement again, and I turned around. I was too annoyed at the world in general to wait for a response. I didn't mean to storm off, but I think that's what I may have done.

TWENTY-FOUR

I couldn't sleep. I replayed my conversation with Jack over and over again, remembering the way his eyes sparkled and the perfect angles of his face.

Thoughts of the cupcake I hadn't even ordered, never mind eaten, kept haunting me. Should I go down to the café again and order myself one? But then Jack would see me through his security system, eating a triple chocolate cupcake all by myself, and he might think that was an invitation to come and talk to me again. Even worse, I might spend half an hour eating that damn cupcake, and Jack would ignore me and *not* come and talk to me.

Of course, there was always the possibility that Jack had knocked off work, and wouldn't even see me go down for that cupcake.

I groaned, feeling like I was in high school all over again. Except this time, I knew just what to do. I pulled up the room service menu, dialed the number, and ordered a cupcake to be brought up to my room.

I'd just finished my treat when there was a knock on the door.

I peered out through the fisheye, narrowed my eyes and opened the door.

"I'm sorry if I was rude earlier," Jack said. "I didn't mean to offend you, or offer you a bribe. Not that I've got any reason to bribe you."

"Hmm."

I looked at him suspiciously. In my experience, men usually aren't quick to apologize – especially if they don't really have anything to apologize *for*.

"Never mind," I said gruffly.

Jack was standing close enough that I could smell his oceanic cologne, and I wondered distractedly what brand he wore. It was far too late to be talking with a man this good looking.

I was about to mutter a polite-ish goodnight and slam the door, when Jack said, "What're your plans for tomorrow?"

"How do you mean?"

"Any suspects you need to badger, neighbors you need to drag around? Innocent people you need to accuse of crimes?"

I smiled. Criminal or not, it was hard not to smile at Jack. "Are you calling yourself innocent?"

"I've been taught by my lawyers to never respond to that question."

"We're working on a good lead," I bluffed.

"So, maybe you could take the day off, tomorrow? It *is* Saturday, after all."

"Maybe," I said. "Why?"

Jack shrugged. "I thought I'd try to help you out. You're investigating a stolen Van Gogh, you might as well check out one of the largest Van Gogh collections. Might help you better understand the, uh, *motivations* of the burglar."

I looked at him. It didn't seem like a bad idea, but..."I can go by myself."

Jack shook his head, and I wondered fleetingly if he knew I'd ordered the cupcake. Not that it mattered.

"It's a private collection," he said. "I need to go with you, to get you in."

I watched him closely, trying to read the gaps in his expression, but if he was hiding something, I couldn't find it.

The desire to see some Van Goghs overcame the suspicions I had about Jack. And ok, maybe I was growing used to this proximity and wanted more of it. "Fine. But I don't want to spend too long."

"It'll take all day," Jack said. "It's pretty far from here."

"Don't *you* have work?"

"I worked all of last night, and I can take time off. Come on."

"Now?"

Jack looked at me and the corners of his mouth up. His upper lip had an exquisite curve to it, and I wondered what it would feel like to kiss that curve.

"It's a long journey," he said. "If you want to see it, we need to leave right away."

I grabbed my purse and followed him out. I didn't quite know where we were going, but the cavewoman part of my brain had taken control again. "Follow attractive man," she said, and that's what I was doing. I was just lucky she hadn't said, "Drag attractive man into cave. Now."

———

"WHERE ARE WE going?" I asked.

Jack and I were sitting in the back of a black Town Car being driven by a big man with tattoos on his neck, and I was starting

177

to wonder if going on a longish trip with Jack was such a good idea after all.

"First stop," Jack said, just as the car pulled up to the curb. "Is your condo."

"Oh." I looked up at the familiar building. "This seems like third-date kinda stuff." The words were out before I could stop them, and I added quickly, "Or third-month. Whatever."

Jack looked amused. "We need to grab your passport. I can wait out in the hall if you'd prefer."

"Grab him now!" the cavewoman in my head was telling me. The rest of me was thinking about Mrs. Weebly.

"That's ok," I told Jack. "I don't want Mrs. Weebly to get you."

Jack raised one eyebrow. "The seductress next door?"

I frowned. "Grumpy old lady."

"I'm great with old ladies! I'm sure she'll love me."

"Not this one."

As we headed toward my condo, we passed Ian's door with its deep gash left by Mr. Beard's knife.

I turned to Jack. "I should check on Ian," I said, and knocked.

I'd been expecting Ian to come bounding over and open the door within seconds, but it took almost a minute. He was wearing light-blue, Spiderman-print pajamas, and was rubbing his eyes sleepily.

He brightened when he saw me. "Oh, hi!"

"Hey, Ian. I hope we didn't wake you?" He shook his head sleepily, and I said, "You still have the knife Mr. Beard stuck into your door, right?" He nodded again. "Someone from the police department'll stop by and pick it up."

His shoulders slumped and I detected the hint of a pout. "Why?"

178

"Dusting for prints."

"I was hoping to keep it. Souvenir."

"Maybe they'll give it back," I told him, trying not to roll my eyes. "You didn't notice anything unusual after I left, did you?"

"No, sorry. Who's your friend?"

"This is Jack," I told Ian. "We were just heading to my place to get my passport."

"I'll come with," Ian said, and closed the door behind himself. "Where are you going?"

"Somewhere with fancy security," Jack told him.

"Is this PI business?" Ian asked me. "Are you two working together? I thought *we'd* be working together."

I opened the door to my condo and stepped in. The big paper with "Surprise!" written on it in crayon was still lying on the floor, so I picked it up, crumpled it into a ball and threw it away.

"Remains of a surprise party?" Jack asked curiously, and I shook my head.

"You don't want to know."

I gave Ian a warning glance, and standing behind Jack, Ian mimed zipping his lips and throwing the key.

I found my passport, and we all walked out.

"I'll see you later," I told Ian, not really sure if I meant it, and Jack and I got back into his car.

———

JACK'S CAR SPED north, and I said, "Where are we going?"

Jack smiled. "It's a surprise. I promise it'll be a much better one than whatever that paper on your floor meant."

I looked at him warily. Almost any surprise would be better than Mr. Beard jumping out of my bedroom holding a knife, but I was still wondering if I'd made the right choice in going along with Jack.

I pulled out my phone, deciding to let someone know I was going away with Jack. But who? My mother would start praying that I was eloping with someone, Nanna would think I should've taken her along. My dad wouldn't care, and Emily might start doing a background check on Jack. Finally, I texted Stone.

He called me back thirty seconds after I'd sent the text.

"Yo," he said. "Whereabouts is this guy taking you?"

"I'm not sure. That's why I texted you."

Stone was silent for a few seconds and then said, "I ran his background after dinner last night. He's a decent guy. Pillar of society and all that."

I gulped. Somehow, I didn't feel at all reassured to know that Stone had looked into this guy.

"He's a playboy, though," Stone continued. "So don't fall for him."

He hung up, and I sat there feeling dejected.

"You don't look very happy," Jack said. "Who was that?"

I shook my head and tried to put Stone's warning out my mind.

———

"I HOPE WE'RE just going to Mexico," I said nervously, as I waited with Jack.

We'd driven up to a door in McCarran Airport that I'd never even noticed before, let alone been through. Inside, there was a plush lobby, a cafeteria serving free food, and what looked like work stations. A woman dressed in an expensive-looking business suit had taken our passports and told us she'd do the paperwork.

Jack looked at me closely. "You're not scared of flying, are you?"

I shook my head. I was more scared of being outside the USA with a man I'd just met. *It's not too late to turn around and leave*, I told myself. But some perverse instinct made me stick around, desperate to find out where we were going.

The woman who'd taken our passports came back after a few minutes, and ushered us over to another door, where three men dressed in white pilots' uniforms were waiting for us. Jack introduced them to me as Darren, our pilot, and James and Roy, our co-pilots. It was then that I realized we'd be flying on Jack's private jet, and we followed the three men over to the plane.

"So, you've never flown commercial?" I asked Jack, once we were inside.

I was trying to act cool and not be overwhelmed by the size and luxuriousness of the plane. The cabin was large enough to fit fifty people comfortably, but there were only ten seats. Everything was cream – the walls, the leather seats, the plush carpeting – and outside the tiny windows, I could see the runway stretching out before us.

Jack smiled. "I've flown commercial most of my life. But now I need something that gets me places on short notice."

I settled down in one of the plush seats, unable to stop thinking that this would make a great getaway vehicle.

Jack sat on the seat across the aisle. "There's food in the kitchenette behind," he said. "I hope you won't mind if I get some sleep. It was a long night."

"Of course."

I watched him press some buttons, and his chair reclined into a flat bad, and then a screen slid up, blocking my view.

I wasn't going to waste my time on my first – and maybe only – flight on a private jet. I wanted to wander around, find out what was in the kitchenette, maybe see if I could get into the cockpit and learn something about flying. But first, I pressed the buttons on the arm of my chair, just to see what they did.

The chair reclined, the seat went up, and before I knew it, my eyes closed and I drifted off to sleep.

———

"Tiffany, tiffany, wake up."

Jack's voice floated over to me across the aisle, and I found myself trying to focus. A few seconds later, I was rubbing my eyes, remembering I was in a private jet, and I didn't know where I was flying to.

"Oh, good, you're up." Jack sounded relieved, and I lowered the partition and looked over. "We're going to land in a bit," he said. "You might want to eat something."

As if on cue, I felt a stab of hunger. I checked my wrist, but I hadn't worn my watch this morning. "What time is it?"

"Lunchtime," Jack said, and I smiled and headed over to the kitchenette. "There's a chocolate cupcake from The Tremonte café in the fridge," he called out. "Just in case."

Half an hour later, I'd stuffed myself with gourmet sandwiches and the cupcake, and the plane was descending. The sky outside was a bright, sunny blue. I checked the time on my phone and paled.

"The flight took *twelve hours*," I said. "Where the hell are we?"

The plane bumped down onto the runway and began to taxi over to the gate.

Jack smiled. "Welcome to Amsterdam."

I stared at him, aghast. "You brought me to Amsterdam?"

"Surprise!"

The plane slowed down and stopped, and the pilot came over to open the door. I tried not to scream, but my anger was bubbling up inside. A woman in a navy blue pantsuit was waiting for us on the other side of the door, and she escorted us through security.

I stayed silent, not wanting to cause a scene in a foreign airport. Who knew how the grim-looking Dutch officials would react to a crazy American girl causing a fuss? Maybe they'd arrest me, or maybe they'd send me to the tiny airport interrogation room I keep reading about in the news, and it'd be *days* before I could get back to Vegas. It was probably better to stay with Jack, and convince him to take me back home as soon as possible.

Once out of the airport, we got into the back of another Town Car. This time, the chauffeur was a slim, blond man who introduced himself as Lars. We drove through streets bisected by tram lines, and crossed tiny, picturesque canals. Numerous cyclists rode past us, and half the buildings had signs in Dutch, words that I couldn't understand.

"How'd you like Amsterdam?" Jack asked.

I pushed a button to slide up the privacy partition between us and the chauffeur, and turned to Jack.

"This isn't funny," I said, trying to sound calm and collected, despite my anger. "I thought we were maybe going to Mexico. I don't want to be in Amsterdam! You can't just fly someone here without any warning! It's not normal!"

Jack's green eyes glinted. "I'm not normal."

A sliver of fear shot through my heart. "You're not going to kill me and leave me here are you? Or sell me into white slavery?"

I was too angry to be really scared, and Jack laughed. "Don't be silly. I thought you'd like it, you said you wanted to see some Van Goghs."

"Yeah, somewhere near Vegas. Not half-way across the world." And then I realized. "You thought this would be a great bribe."

Jack shook his head. "No, I thought this would be a great date."

I stared at him. "You want to date me?"

"Of course I do."

I was surprised and flattered for only a split second, and then my anger returned with a vengeance and I crossed my arms against my chest. "This isn't a date. You can't just drag someone somewhere and call it a date. And I don't want to date you."

Jack raised one eyebrow. "You don't?"

The rational part of me was silently screaming to shut up. But I didn't.

"I don't," I told him. "I think you're behind the Van Gogh theft and I don't want to date a criminal."

"I'm not a criminal. My lawyers will tell you that."

I glared at him, about to tell him just what I thought of him and his lawyers, when my phone rang. It was Stone.

"What?" I said, sounding more annoyed than I meant to.

"Do you know you're in Amsterdam?"

He sounded surprised and I scowled. "Yes, of course I know! How do you know?"

"Remember how, during the Ethan Becker murder investigation, I installed tracking software on your phone? I said I'd taken it off, but I didn't."

I inhaled sharply. "I *cannot* believe you! That is *such* an invasion of privacy!"

"It saved your life, once."

"I don't care! I mean, I do, but you need to stop tracking me! I can take care of myself! And I have a new bodyguard now, Ian."

Stone was silent for a few seconds and then he said, "Fine. I hope Ian's experienced?"

"Of course he is," I fibbed. "Why don't you leave me to deal with my life?"

I regretted the words as soon as they were out of my mouth. Stone's been a good friend to me, and he's looked out for me more than I deserved. He'd just called at the wrong time.

"Ok," Stone said. "Have a good time in Amsterdam. Call me if you need anything."

He hung up, and I looked at the phone sadly, wishing I hadn't yelled at Stone.

Beside me, Jack was silent for a few minutes, and then he said, "Who was that?"

"Just a friend."

I didn't feel like explaining, and Jack didn't press it.

The phone rang again, and I looked down. It wasn't a number I knew, so I decided to save some money on roaming fees and not answer it.

"How long are we staying here?" I asked Jack. "I didn't pack anything."

"I thought we'd go through the museum and leave, in which case we'll be back in Vegas tonight. Unless you want to stay longer, of course."

I shook my head. Leaving Vegas and flying to Amsterdam was crazy. I wasn't sure how I felt about the whole thing yet, but I knew I didn't want to stay overnight.

We pulled up in front of a large building whose side was covered with blown up replicas of Van Gogh's most famous works, and as we stepped out of the car, I reminded Jack, "This isn't a date."

"I understand that," he said, and I followed him as we bypassed the line, showed the guard our passports, and stepped inside.

"There's no-one else here," I said, looking around.

Jack grinned. "I booked out the whole place for us."

I tried not to feel overwhelmed. This would've been a great date if it *was* a date.

"This isn't a date," I said, more for my own benefit than Jack's.

He smiled and we looked over at a smartly dressed brunette walking toward us.

"I am Carina," she told us, with a slightly Eastern European accent, "I will guide you through the museum today." She turned to Jack and said, "Thank you for your generous support of the foundation."

Jack replied gracefully, while I thought to myself, *What foundation?* The things I didn't know about Jack Weber seemed to be endless.

TWENTY-FIVE

I felt slightly exhausted as the plane took off and I was pushed back against my seat.

The last three hours had been one long walk through the museum, listening to Carina discuss interesting facts about the artist's life and his style of art, coupled with the overwhelming sensation of seeing so many gorgeous paintings all at once.

"That was fun," I told Jack weakly, unable to get over my sheer disbelief of what we'd just done.

"Thanks. Maybe we'll do it again sometime? Another day, another trip?"

I looked into his eyes and an involuntary shiver ran through my body. The man was mind-blowingly handsome, wealthier than anyone I'd met, and he wanted to spend that wealth doing fun things with me. His dark green eyes stared into mine with a mixture of confidence and hope. More than anything else, I wanted to say "yes" to his offer.

But I shook my head. "I'm pretty sure you're a criminal," I said, as much to myself as to him, and he leaned back in his seat with a smile.

The plane had finished its ascent, and was now cruising steadily. Jack said, "Isn't being a private investigator all about being open to different explanations of what might've happened?"

"It is, but right now, all explanations point toward you."

Jack shook his head. "How'd you become a PI, anyway?"

I smiled. "How'd you become such a successful businessman?"

"I asked you first."

"What is this, first grade?"

"You started it."

"Did not."

We smiled at each other, and Jack began to tell me about his work. He'd gotten into the casino business by accident – he'd started out as a valet, managing his own investments on the side. But over time, his investments did better, his company grew, and he wound up buying large shares in casinos.

I was surprised that he hadn't been born into money. His parents had been immigrants from Germany, and he'd gone to public schools all his life.

"It's your turn now," he said, after a while. I didn't have any excuse for being secretive – or any reason, really, so I told him about being a casino dealer who was trying to get more meaningful work as an investigator.

He listened thoughtfully for a while, and then he said, "You know, I've got a pile of books, up front. There's an autobiography of a woman who used to be a PI, you might find it interesting."

I headed toward the shelf he was indicating, and pawed through the piled-up books.

"Why do you have these here?" I asked, holding up two Harlequin romances. I smiled to myself as I imagined Jack reading them. There were at least six more in the pile.

Jack smiled back, and I was struck once again by how charming his smile was. "Sometimes I have female friends riding on the plane with me. Those are for them."

"Oh." I turned around so he couldn't see my expression, and put the books down quickly. Once I found the PI's autobiography, I headed back to my seat, and pretended to read it, while thinking about all those Harlequin-reading "female friends" that rode on Jack's plane with him.

TWENTY-SIX

"I 'll grab my stuff and head home," I said to Jack as I stepped out in front of The Tremonte. It was just past two in the morning, and Vegas casino-life was in full swing. Tourists wearing shorts and brightly printed shirts walked in and out of the casinos along the Strip, gawking at the lights and, depending on how their run at the games had been, either grinning maniacally or looking like their dog had died.

Jack gave me a skeptical look. "The room's already paid for. You might as well stay and enjoy the breakfast buffet tomorrow."

We stepped inside and the air conditioning hit us, reminding me of the temperature in Amsterdam. Ever since he'd told me about his Harlequin-reading "women friends," I'd been eager to get away from Jack, but he did have a point. And the siren song of the breakfast buffet was irresistible.

I stifled my sigh. "You're right."

As we headed past the lobby, Sam Rampell, the director of Casino Kings, stepped out of the casino with a scowl on his face. The moment he saw us, the scowl disappeared, replaced by a glimmer of surprise when he saw me with Jack. And then the surprise was replaced with a suave, polite friendliness.

"Jack," he said, coming over to us. "You're just the man I needed to see. We need to talk about the talent."

Sam nodded at me politely, and the two men began discussing production costs, actors and the cost to the casino. I tuned out for a few moments, wondering if I should just excuse myself and head to my room. I couldn't stay on at The Tremonte indefinitely, but I still hadn't figured out what to do about Mr. Beard. Maybe I could ask Ian to come over to my place and sleep on the couch…

The conversation seemed to be winding down, and then Sam said, "Jack, would you mind if I had a word with Tiffany in private?"

"No, of course not. I was about to head upstairs and get back to work." He looked at me inquisitively. "If that's ok with you?"

"Of course." I looked at him awkwardly. "Thanks for a lovely time, today."

One corner of Jack's mouth went up and his eyes looked into mine. "It *was* nice," he said. "Thank you."

He turned and walked away, and I watched him for a few seconds. Next to me, Sam asked, "Did you two just come back from dinner?"

"No. Museum visit."

The goodbye would've been a lot more awkward if Sam hadn't been there. Maybe Jack would've kissed me. Of course, I'd told him it wasn't a date. My mind began to wander and I imagined how it would be to kiss him.

"So…" Sam was saying slowly. "You two are a thing now."

I snapped back to reality. "No, we're not. We're just friends. Not even friends really." I shook my head. "I'm just investigating him for something."

Sam was watching me closely. "Crystal's murder?"

"No, something else."

Sam raised one eyebrow. "He's involved in another crime? He's financing a lot of this movie, should I be concerned?"

I shook my head again. "No." I was feeling strangely defensive of Jack, but I couldn't think of a good explanation. "It's just…this random thing. Nothing important."

"Right." Sam nodded. "And how's the investigation into Crystal's death going?"

I made a "so-so" face.

"Well, I'm sure you'll find something."

He smiled at me politely, and suddenly I felt a flash of annoyance. Sam must've thought I was a clueless Vegas dealer with no investigative skills whatsoever, and you know what? He might've been right. Still, I didn't want him to believe that I hadn't gotten anywhere with the investigation yet, so I fibbed, "I've got a good lead. There was a guy who was constantly hitting on Crystal – her friends think this guy had something to do with her death."

"Oh." He looked at me thoughtfully and ran a hand through his hair. "I had no idea – I mean. I know who it was, I just didn't think he was – didn't think he had…"

He looked at me seriously and his voice trailed off.

"Who was the guy?" I asked.

Sam leaned forward and said in a low voice, "Crystal told me it was Jack."

Time seemed to slow down. I could see Sam's dark, serious eyes, and the lights of the casino pit behind him. There was a jangling noise like coins pouring into a pot, and then the sharp sirens of a jackpot win. Around us, people were walking up and down, chatting with each other.

I said weakly, "She told you it was Jack?"

He nodded. "I didn't tell you earlier because I thought someone else would mention it before me. Jack's women are his business, and I really need his funding."

I nodded, as though what he'd just said made sense, but I was only half present. The rest of me was wondering what the hell Jack had been doing with Crystal. It was bad enough that he had women friends who rode on his private jet with him so frequently that he kept books for them. Maybe Crystal read Harlequin romances. She seemed the type.

I gave myself a tiny shake – I was jealous of dead woman. And maybe Sam was wrong about the two of them being together. Yes, that made sense. The man had thought Jack and I were together, when clearly we weren't. So he must be wrong about Crystal.

"Did you ever see them together?" I asked. "Jack told me he never came on set."

"No, he didn't," Sam said thoughtfully. "Come to think of it, I never saw them together inside the casino, but I think I saw them having dinner once, some place downtown. And the day before Crystal died, they were standing outside on the Strip, arguing about something."

My stomach clenched sharply. Jack had told me he didn't know Crystal, and like a fool, I'd believed him. "Did you hear what they were arguing about?"

"No, I was too far away. I don't think they saw me."

I nodded. "Well, thanks for telling me this."

"Of course. I hope you'll keep it confidential?"

I forced myself to smile. "I'd be a terrible PI if I didn't."

I'd already been a terrible PI. I'd trusted Jack; I'd come close to believing that he had nothing to do with the theft. I felt sick thinking that I'd gone to Amsterdam with him – maybe if I'd kicked up a bigger fuss, if I'd told him that the Ferrari number-plate trace linked him to the scene, he would've killed me and dumped my body in one of those picturesque canals.

Just like he'd killed Crystal and dumped her body in one of the streets of North Vegas.

TWENTY-SEVEN

B y the time I got to my room and closed the door behind me, I was feeling numb inside. I refused to let myself explore the emotions bubbling within me. I'd been played, and I'd come so close to believing that Jack was a nice guy. My memory pulled up images of his charming smile and his dazzling good looks, and I realized he was a textbook sociopath. And I was staying in his hotel.

I hung the "Do Not Disturb" sign on the door, and drew the security chain across. The room was large and well-lit, and the windows reflected it back to me. The silence was almost unbearable, so I switched on the TV. But then I wouldn't be able to hear anyone approaching. I switched it off again.

My heart was thumping wildly. I checked the windows – they were locked now, but could be unlocked and slid open. I heard footsteps outside in the hall and froze. But then the footsteps passed my room and went away. I breathed again.

I sat down on the edge of the bed, exhausted and unable to think straight. The in-room phone rang and I jumped up.

The caller ID said, "Reception," and I stared at it; I could just not answer. But then Jack would try my cellphone, or worse, he might come to the door.

I picked up, and stayed on the line while the receptionist transferred the call across to Jack.

"Sorry about getting waylaid by Sam," Jack said. "Just wanted to make sure you made it to the room ok."

"Yes." I closed my eyes weakly, knowing he'd seen me come up on the security cameras.

"You sound tired," he said.

"I am. Thanks for a fun day." And then inspiration hit. "I'm sorry I thought you were a criminal. You seem like a nice guy." If Jack didn't think I suspected him of anything, maybe he wouldn't bother me.

There was a pause at the other end, and then Jack said, "Really?"

He sounded suspicious, so I decided to add a bright smile to my voice. "Of course! Today was wonderful."

"Oh." He still didn't seem to believe me and said, "Maybe we can go out again, sometime."

"Uh. I'm not ready to date anyone now."

"Bullshit." The answer was sharp and sudden. "I don't think you really trust me."

"I, uh, no…" My heart raced furiously, and I couldn't think of a good excuse.

Jack sighed, and when he spoke again, he sounded tired and dejected. "Never mind. It's too late, and I can't change what I did."

He hung up, and I stared at the receiver. What had Jack done? Why was he admitting to something now? I glanced at the door, and then at the large, floor-to-ceiling windows. I didn't want to sleep in here. And I definitely didn't want to die in here.

TWENTY-EIGHT

I called the one person in the world I knew could keep me safe, no matter what.

"I'm sorry I yelled at you earlier," I said, when Stone picked up.

He was silent for a few seconds and then he said, "How was the date?"

I didn't have the energy to scowl. "It wasn't a date."

There was some more silence. Stone said, "Your voice sounds funny. Are you ok?"

"I'm fine. What're you up to, tonight?"

"Finishing up at the office. Do you need anything?"

"Some company would be nice. I don't feel safe in my room."

"No-one can get past those Tremonte security cameras. Mr. Beard's worked in a casino long enough to stay away from there."

"It's not Mr. Beard."

There was another long silence, as Stone thought things out. Finally, he said, "And this guy doesn't worry about security cameras?"

"No."

"Go downstairs. Stay in a public spot."

If I went downstairs and sat by myself, Jack might come and talk to me. But on the bright side, he couldn't murder me out in public.

I took a deep breath and said, "Will you come and have coffee with me?"

"Is this an apology coffee?"

I smiled. "Yes. And an apology meal, if you'd like. I haven't had dinner yet."

———

STONE DIDN'T EAT anything. But he had three mugs of coffee as he sat in the café and watched me go through two club sandwiches. I couldn't bring myself to order the triple chocolate cupcake because it reminded me of Jack and made me feel sick.

But Jack had nothing to do with any of the other flavors. So I had an orange-lemon cupcake with vanilla frosting, and offered half to Stone. He shook his head, like I'd known he would; it was the only reason I'd offered him some in the first place.

We sat there for a bit over an hour, me devouring and Stone watching. He was cocooned in silence, and I didn't feel like talking.

After a while, he said, "Do you want to go somewhere else?"

I looked up at him, amazed. "That's a brilliant idea! Why didn't I think of it?'

He shrugged. "Maybe because you're so scared. Want to tell me what's going on?"

I shook my head. "I haven't figured it out completely, yet."

Stone nodded, and I settled the bill and followed him out to The Treasury Casino, next door. It was strange, going there when I didn't have a shift, but it seemed like the easiest option.

I settled down at the café, and had another coffee with Stone, before I told him to go home.

"I should be fine here," I said, and he nodded and left me alone.

TWENTY-NINE

I stumbled back to The Tremonte at seven o'clock. The night wasn't yet over for the gamblers in the pit, but it *was* over for me.

I hated having to pull an all-nighter when I didn't have a shift. But I'd make the most of today – I'd head home and take a nap, and then maybe go talk to Ben, the other co-producer. I wasn't sure what I'd do after that, but I knew I didn't want to spend time at The Tremonte.

I packed my bag and took the elevator down to the lobby, and when I stepped out, Jack was waiting for me.

He looked grim, his face as handsome as ever, but his eyes were serious and worried. I took a step back when I saw him, and looked around. There were lots of people nearby. I was safe.

"What's wrong?" he said, coming forward. "Why are you leaving? The breakfast buffet just opened."

I looked away from him and tried to take a few steps toward the lobby. "I'm not feeling hungry."

"Then just have a coffee. We've got delicious scrambled eggs and smoked salmon." I shook my head but he went on, "I'm having breakfast now. Join me. Please."

I looked up at him. He was turning on the charm again, the smile as captivating as ever, but all I could see was a psychopath trying to snare me.

On the other hand, how could I spend the rest of my life running away from Jack Weber? He had money and contacts, and knew how to put them to good use. My best bet was to have breakfast with him, and try to convince him that he had nothing to worry about from me.

We headed over to the breakfast room, which was already packed with tourists gorging themselves on platefuls of greasy food. We skipped the mile-long line for regular guests and went to the shorter line for VIP guests and those staying in suites. I didn't know if I'd manage to eat, but I loaded up my plate with croissants and sausages and scrambled eggs, grabbed a coffee, and followed Jack to a table in the corner.

We sat across from each other, and he looked at me seriously and said, "I saw you leave the casino with another man last night. I didn't know you had a boyfriend."

I was tempted to lie about Stone being my boyfriend, but that might just lead to more problems. I said, "I'm not sure if he's my boyfriend. It's complicated."

It was a cop-out phrase, but Jack seemed to believe me. "So maybe you'd consider that date?"

"Jack." I shook my head, and picked at my food, before looking back up at him. "I know."

He held my glance for what seemed like eternity but was probably only a few seconds. "Yes," he said finally. "You know."

We chewed away in silence and then Jack said, "But you don't know the whole thing. Or why."

I shook my head. "It's not up to me. Murder is serious business."

Jack frowned. "Murder?"

"Crystal?"

He sat back in his chair and looked at me like I was spout-
ing Latin. Finally, he said, "Are you serious? You think I killed
Crystal?"

I took another bite of the eggs. "Witnesses saw you arguing.
There'll be a DNA match. It's not about me, at this stage."

Jack shook his head. "There won't be a DNA match. I never
even *met* Crystal. Why don't I come over to the station with you
right now and volunteer to do the test?"

I stared at him warily. Either he was very, very stupid, or he
was rich enough to bribe the Medical Examiner.

"So?" he said. "Are we going down to the station now or
not?"

I kept staring at him, imagining the sequence of events. It
was a closed case, so why would they reopen it just to match
Jack's DNA with that found on Crystal? If anything, they'd be
annoyed with me for bothering one of their biggest donors.

I said slowly, "The day before she died, you were seen arguing with her."

Jack shook his head. "I spent the whole day up in my office.
You can check The Tremonte security cameras, if you want."

"The day before she died," I repeated to myself. Why did
that sound familiar?

And then I remembered. Max had said he'd spent the
whole day with Crystal. That they hadn't even stepped out of
the hotel.

I rested my elbows on the table, put my head in my hands
and groaned softly.

It wasn't adding up. Jack could doctor The Tremonte security tapes, but he couldn't doctor The Palazzo tapes. If I checked

at The Palazzo, I'd probably see that Crystal hadn't stepped out that day. Something told me that Jack was telling the truth, too.

I felt my shoulders sag and then my head began to pound. Jack was looking at me concernedly. "You feeling ok?"

I shook my head. I was feeling nauseous. I should be relieved that Jack seemed to not have killed Crystal, but the emotional rollercoaster was leaving me a wreck.

"I'm sorry," I told Jack. "I feel really sick."

I stood up quickly, and Jack followed. "Should I call the casino doctor?"

"No. I think – I think I just need some sleep."

"Let me walk you to your room."

I looked at him warily. Sleeping in The Tremonte meant that Jack might break in and kill me. Sleeping in my apartment meant the Mr. Beard might break in and kill me.

I didn't want to believe that Jack was a killer, but my emotions were all over the place, and I couldn't trust myself to think straight.

"I'm fine," I managed to say. "I should check out and get back to my place."

"Are you sure the re-painting's finished?"

I stared at him blankly.

"Your place was being re-painted, remember?" Jack said, and I nodded.

"Right. Painting. Yep, done."

I picked up my bag and headed toward the lobby.

Jack followed and said, "At least let me comp your room."

"The client's paying," I said, and he didn't say anything more until I completed the paperwork.

"My car can drop you off," Jack said. "You shouldn't walk if you're feeling sick."

I stared at him. The man knew where I lived. If he wanted me out of the way, he could just break into my condo. Him and Mr. Beard, both.

I shook my head. "Maybe the walk'll clear my head."

Jack looked at me suspiciously, but I was already walking quickly toward the front doors, as though moving faster would help me get to safety.

THIRTY

"I'm glad you're home," I told Ian, stepping in quickly and shutting the door behind me. "You look like a mess."

He ran one hand through his hair and yawned. "You woke me up." And then his face brightened. "What's the rush, have you found a big clue? Do you need me to come along?"

I looked at him and then walked past and peeked into his bedroom.

He was as messy as a teenager. There were clothes on the floor, and the robot-print bedsheets looked like they hadn't been washed in months. But the window was open a crack, and the room didn't smell too bad.

"What're you looking for?" Ian asked from behind me. "If you tell me I can find it. I know my room's a mess, but I didn't know you'd be looking in."

I walked over to the bed, sat down, and placed my bag on the floor.

"I need a place to sleep," I said. "People might break into my place. Can I sleep here?"

Ian nodded quickly. "Of course. We're partners, partners help each other out."

I sighed. "We're not partners yet."

"But we will be. An officer came by yesterday and I gave him the knife for you. If we weren't partners, I might've kept it for myself."

I was too tired to argue. "I'm a light sleeper," I told Ian. "You're not going to try any funny business, are you?"

He looked offended. "Of course not! We're partners, you don't double-cross your partner." He lifted his chin. "I watched five Bogart movies last night. I'm gonna be just like him. You'll see."

I sighed and slipped off my shoes. "Good for you. I'll be up in a few hours."

I lay down on the bed. His pillow was lumpy and soft, and the mattress sunk under my weight.

"Do you need me to do anything?" Ian asked.

"Keep an eye out on my condo," I said drowsily.

"Great idea, pardner."

He left the room, and I let my exhaustion take over. I knew that it wasn't a question of *if* someone tried to break into my condo – just *who*.

⌇

I WOKE UP to the sound of Loony Tunes and groaned. I'd only been asleep for a few hours, and my head hurt. I stumbled out the room and glared at Ian.

"That's really loud."

He was slouched over on the couch, chomping on Froot Loops and laughing at Daffy Duck.

"Sorry," he said. "I forgot you were a light sleeper."

I looked around his kitchen. There was a nifty-looking Nespresso machine, and I said, "Where're the pods?"

Ian left his cartoons and came over to find the pods, inserted one and pressed a button to make the coffee.

"Did you see anyone breaking into my condo?" I asked, and he looked sheepish.

"Well…There was this episode of *Castle* on. I had to watch it since I'm learning about detecting and I'm trying to be like Bogart. And then Looney Tunes came on."

"So that's a no. You have no idea if anyone tried to break in."

He looked at me apologetically, his eyes round and dejected. I sighed. He was too puppy-like to get angry with, plus he'd made me coffee.

I took a few sips and said, "You don't have any cupcakes here, do you?"

He shook his head, and I took a long sip of the coffee. "Fine. I've got cupcakes in my fridge, so I'll head back to my apartment now."

"I'll come with," Ian said quickly. "I can be your bodyguard."

I looked at him slowly.

"Please," he said. "I'll be really good at it, I promise."

I rolled my eyes. "Ok. But no Looney Tunes."

"Deal."

I grabbed my bag and walked down the hall. I unlocked my door, pushed it open in front of me and peered inside – there was nobody in the living area, the dining space or the kitchen. There were no envelopes or poster-papers bearing messages lying on the floor. The windows looked like they hadn't been tampered with. All good signs.

I took a deep breath and stepped in. Ian stepped in too, crowding behind me.

I pointed at the ground, and mouthed, "Wait here."

Ian nodded frantically.

I stepped slowly toward the bedroom. The condo was quiet, and I could hear someone else's TV from down the hallway. I peered around the doorway and into the bedroom. It was dark, and cool and empty. I glanced longingly at the bed – the sheets looked smooth and clean and crisp. Too bad I couldn't have slept here. But the walk home hadn't cleared out my mind and the only good idea I could come up with was to crash at Ian's.

I checked under the bed, stepped into the bathroom and looked around, and opened the closet door. All empty.

I pulled the curtains apart with one sweeping motion. There was nobody on the tiny balcony. I closed my eyes in relief.

"You can close the door," I called to Ian, and sighed at the bed, which tried to entice me. Should I take another nap? Probably not, I decided.

I heard Ian closing the door and he said, "What're we doing today? Are you interviewing someone? You know, I could come if you're interviewing someone. I'm good at interviews."

"Cupcakes first," I said.

I pulled out the box of cupcakes Glen had given me, and opened the lid. I placed one on a plate for me, and one on a plate for Ian. We ate our cupcakes in silence, and then I had another one. I was starting to think more clearly, and the more I thought about it, the more things seemed to make sense.

Sam said he'd seen Jack arguing with someone on the Strip, the day before Crystal died. But it couldn't be Crystal, because she hadn't stepped out of The Palazzo that day. Jack claimed he hadn't stepped out of work. But maybe he had, and he'd been arguing with someone who looked like Crystal. Or, more likely, Sam had been standing too far away to recognize either of them properly.

Crystal's body had been found near Ben McAllister's house. And he was the one person I hadn't talked to yet – he'd been conveniently out of town for the whole week. It was high time I spoke to him.

"Have you ever interviewed someone?" I asked Ian.

"No. But I reckon I'll be good. I'm really good at talking to people, and I've seen lots of cop shows. I know how it's done."

I looked at him and pulled out my phone. "I do have an interview," I said. "And you can come along. But you need to be quiet, and let me do the talking."

"Sure," he said.

I should've known better than to believe him.

THIRTY-ONE

Ben McAllister said he was free to talk to me for the next two hours, and he suggested we meet in the café at The Tremonte.

"That's ok," I said. "You can skip the travel time; I can come to your cousin's place in North Vegas."

He was silent for a second and I continued, "That's where you're staying, right? It'll give me a chance to drop by the murder site after we talk."

"Ok," he said. "We can talk here."

He gave me the address, and Ian and I headed over and pulled up to a swanky, white house. It was double-storied and had pillars in front, and looked like it would have a pool in the back.

I was half-expecting a maid in a black-and white uniform to open the door, so I almost took a step back when a slightly chubby man with wavy blond hair opened the door.

"Tiffany Black?" he said.

I nodded. "You must be Ben."

"Come in." And then he noticed Ian. "Who's this?"

"I'm Ian Ewanson," Ian said. "I'm her partner. I heard you were trying to sleep with Crystal Macombe."

I closed my eyes and groaned. "I'm sorry about him," I said, regretting the information I'd slipped to Ian. "I really am."

When I opened my eyes I saw that Ben was smiling thinly, and he waved us into a formal sitting room. The house had obviously been built and designed by someone who wanted to impress, but wasn't sure how to do it. A large tri-color abstract painting hung on one wall, its greens and yellows picked up by the green sofa with its yellow cushions.

"Nice décor," I said as I sat down and gave Ian a look that I hoped said, "Shut. Up."

Ben looked at the furniture and painting and said, "My cousin's ex-wife."

I nodded. That made sense.

"Anyway," I said. "What can you tell me about Crystal?"

"Lovely girl," Ben said. "Very friendly. Talented."

Ian said, "Is that why you were trying to sleep with her?"

Ian was sitting too far away for me to kick him, but I glared sternly and said, "Ian," in a warning tone. Ian winked at me, oblivious.

I looked at Ben, who was watching us carefully and said, "How come you're staying in your cousin's place instead of one of the casinos?"

He shrugged. "We're friends. He's got a hot-tub and we help each other get the ladies."

"Like Crystal," Ian said.

I sighed, and Ben rolled his eyes.

"I'm sorry," I said. "But you do have a bit of a reputation on the set."

He raised his hands. "I like women. Is that a crime?"

"No, but not co-operating with the police during a murder investigation is. Why didn't you tell them that Crystal had come to see you just before she was killed?" It was a shot in the dark, but Ben stiffened, and I knew I was right. "Did you kill her and dump her body nearby?" I continued, "Or did you chase her when she ran away?"

We stared at each other for a few seconds, and I was thankful that Ian was silent. Finally, Ben said, "I had nothing to do with her death."

"Then why was she here?"

He looked at me sullenly and after a few seconds, he said, "She wanted to talk about something."

"Like what? Like needing to sleep with you to get the part?"

His eyes narrowed and he said icily, "Nobody *has* to sleep with me to get anything."

"But Crystal thought she did."

"She was wrong. Anyway, I didn't want to sleep with her. She wasn't my type."

"Hunh," I said. "From what I hear, everyone's your type."

We stared at each other, neither willing to talk. And then Ian said, "This house must be a real chick-magnet."

Ben smiled at him. "Yeah." And then he looked at me pointedly. "I don't need any help with the ladies."

"Then what was Crystal doing here that night?" I asked.

"She came to talk to me. She said she knew I had contacts, would I help her get a role somewhere else if she couldn't get this role."

"What did you say?"

Ben shrugged. "I said, sure. But she was going to get this part. Sam was convinced she'd be a star."

I looked from Ben to Ian, and then back at Ben.

Ian stuck his chin out and said, "Why don't we sort this out quickly?" I frowned at him, but it was no use and he went on,

"There was DNA on Crystal's body. Why don't you come down to the station with us and give us a blood sample?"

I groaned inside, imagining the detectives' reactions when I drove up and demanded that the ME take Ben's blood sample.

Ben said, "Sure. I've got no problem with that, because I never touched her. And I definitely didn't kill her."

He sounded convincing, but I wondered if it was a bluff. Maybe he knew that we couldn't get the ME to test his DNA.

"I don't think you're telling the truth about Crystal," I said slowly. "I think you asked Crystal to come over here so you could seduce her. But then, when she said no, you got angry and killed her. Maybe she walked down the street, and you followed her out and killed her there."

Ben shook his head. "Even if I did want to seduce her, why would I kill her if she said no? I can get any girl I want. So one woman says no, big deal."

I looked at him carefully. He was right; the story didn't add up, but I still said, "I don't know why you'd kill her. Maybe your ego was hurt?"

"No," Ben said. "She came over to talk to me. I did try to put the moves on her. Asked if she wanted to go out to the hot-tub. But she said she had a boyfriend, and I let it go. She'd get the part anyway, and I didn't want things to be awkward between us."

"I thought you were the producer. You could just veto her getting the part."

Ben looked at me like I was clueless. Which I probably was, when it came to Hollywood affairs. "It's about money," he said. "Sam thought she'd help make the movie sell. I trusted his judgment."

I nodded, trying to make sense of it.

"Look," Ben said, "We talked for a couple minutes, then she got a phone call. And then a few minutes later, he called again, and she said she had to go."

"Who called?" Ian and I said at the same time.

Ben said, "Sam Rampell."

THIRTY-TWO

The three of us stared at each other, all thinking the same thing. Finally, I said, "We should go. I'll call you if we need you to come in to give that DNA sample."

Ben nodded. "No problem."

Ian and I drove away, and I went straight back to my condo.

"Are we going to talk to Sam, now?" Ian asked, and I looked at him sternly.

"You weren't meant to talk during the interview."

"But I was good. I was like Bogart. I was the bad cop."

"You were rude."

"Yeah, but I got him to talk, didn't I?"

I considered that for a moment, and then I strode out of the carpark and began walking toward The Tremonte. Ian tagged along at my heels, panting slightly at the fast pace.

"I won't talk this time," he said. "I promise."

I couldn't seem to shake him off, and maybe I owed him for letting me sleep over at his place. As we talked, he went on and on about his favorite TV show about mysteries, and how they solved the murders each time.

It was kind of nice to have him talking away, I thought; it stopped me from doing a premature victory dance. And it

215

stopped me from being too ashamed that my thoughts of victory weren't just about discovering Crystal's killer, but also about proving that Jack had nothing to do with her death.

When we got to The Tremonte, Sam was giving directions to a couple having a huge fight. "Really show the despair in your voice," he told the woman. He glanced over to me and went back to work.

I stood beside him quietly, until the scene was over and he was forced to talk to me.

He smiled at me politely. "I'm afraid I'm busy now. Can we talk later?"

I shook my head. "It's a bit urgent, and it'll just take a minute."

Sam sighed, and stepped off the set with me. Ian trailed behind us, and for once, he seemed to be intent on not talking. Maybe he'd exhausted himself on the walk over.

"Sam," I said, when we were standing in a quiet corner where nobody could overhear us. "They found out who killed Crystal."

He looked at me seriously. "Who?"

I continued to stare at him, waiting for him to realize that the game was over.

He waited a few seconds, blinked and then asked me again, "Who?"

"We know it's you," I said.

He took a few seconds to process what I'd just said, and then he tilted his head and smiled. "And why would I do that?"

"I'm not sure," I admitted. "She'd worked for you before, as an extra in two movies. Maybe you fell in love with her." He looked at me skeptically and crossed his arms, but he didn't say anything, so I went on. "You knew she'd gone to Ben's apartment and you thought she was sleeping with him. Why not you? But she kept saying no, and you finally lost your temper. You'd already had a few drinks, and before you knew it, you'd killed her."

"I have an alibi," he said stiffly.

I nodded. "Sure. But I'm sure that when we talk to the people at the bar, we'll find out you left long before midnight."

The charm had left Sam's eyes, and now they were dark and angry. "I don't believe you," he said. "You've got some nerve, coming in here and accusing me of all this."

I shrugged. "Talk's cheap. Why don't we head down to the station and you can give the ME a blood sample and prove you've got nothing to do with all this?"

I watched the blood drain out of Sam's face, and he glanced seriously from Ian to me. "I can't do that," he said, finally. "I'm busy. Stuff to do."

I shrugged. "Suit yourself. We'll have the ME come down to see you."

He took a step back and said something incomprehensible, and I watched him hurry back to the set. I knew what I had to do.

THIRTY-THREE

M y first call was to Emily, who said she'd pass on the information to Detective Coles, and that I'd hear from him soon.

"We got the prints off the knife," she added. "Mr. Beard's
real name is Penrith Goodham."

I laughed drily. "With a name like that, maybe I'd be a criminal, too."

Emily didn't laugh. "Be careful, Tiff," she said. "We'll keep
an eye out for this guy, but you know how short-staffed we are."

My second phone call was to Jack. I asked him if he'd like
to have dinner sometime next week, but he didn't want to wait
till then. "Meet me tonight," he said. "I'm glad we're doing this."

"I've got shifts till Friday. And it's not a date. I don't date
criminals. I just wanted to tell you something I know about the
burglary."

Jack sighed. "Fine. As long as you don't accuse me of
another murder."

"I don't think I will. But, speaking of which, do you think you
could make sure that Sam Rampell can't leave The Tremonte?"

"That might be a bit awkward," Jack said, and I could hear
the smile in his voice. "Is he the one you think killed her, for
now?"

I didn't appreciate being made fun of, so I said, "Yes. And he told me yesterday that he saw you fighting with Crystal. He implied that you killed her."

There was an icy silence, and then Jack said, "I'll make sure he stays put."

I smiled, pleased that my snitching had the desired effect.

———

"ARE YOU SURE it's Sam?" Ian asked as I unlocked my door. "How can you be sure it's Sam?"

"Isn't it obvious?" I asked. "How can you have any doubts?"

"Hey, your answering machine's blinking!"

I was going to do a safety sweep through my condo, but Ian had already walked over to the machine in the corner and pressed a button.

There was one message from three hours ago. "This is Detective Elwood," said the familiar voice. "I've been trying to reach you since yesterday. We really need to talk about the Van Gogh burglary. Call me back."

"Urgh." I was annoyed by the message, and the image of a chubby, suspicious Elwood that popped up in my mind.

"Who's that?" Ian said, as I walked over to the fridge and pulled out the box of cupcakes.

I was going to open it to check how many were left, when Mr. Beard stepped out of the bedroom and into the living area.

The box of cupcakes fell from my hands.

"Surprise!" yelled Mr. Beard. "Isn't this nice?"

His hands were by his side, and I saw that he was holding another knife today. It was almost a relief to see that he hadn't taken Nanna's suggestion and opted for a gun instead. Almost.

Blood pounded in my ears, and I tried not to look into Mr. Beard's eyes. They were tiny and dark and glittering, and behind him, Ian said softly, "Oh. No."

Mr. Beard turned to face Ian, and I took the opportunity to open the cutlery drawer and pull out a knife of my own. The only knives I could see were butter knives and a tiny paring knife, so I picked the paring knife. I wasn't too sure what I could do with it – it didn't seem like a match against Mr. Beard's large chef's knife. But it was better than nothing.

"Go away," Mr. Beard growled at Ian. "This doesn't concern you."

"Y-y-yessir!" Ian said, and he opened the front door. So much for my bodyguard.

Mr. Beard turned toward me and smiled. He said, "I see you're not wearing stilettos, today."

I lifted up my paring knife. "I'm armed," I said, surprised that my voice was steady.

Mr. Beard smiled and lifted his knife to show me. The large blade glinted in the light and I could see that behind him, Ian stood frozen in the doorway.

"Perhaps we should talk," I said quickly. "You know, this whole thing was a misunderstanding."

Mr. Beard took a step toward me, and I lunged and ran toward the bedroom.

"Hey!" Ian shouted, and I was just in time to see him pick a cushion off my couch and throw it at Mr. Beard.

"What the hell!" Mr. Beard turned and stared at Ian in surprise. "Didn't I tell you to scram? Don't make me cut you, too!"

Time slowed down. I saw Mr. Beard raise his knife and step toward Ian. His back was to me, and Ian grabbed another cushion off the couch. This time Ian held it over his chest like a shield. I could see Ian's eyes, large and scared, and his lips seemed to have gone white.

The air felt cold and my arm seemed to rise up on its own. I wasn't thinking when I threw the paring knife at Mr. Beard's neck. It made contact briefly, and then fell to the floor with a soft clang. The three of us stared it, and I froze in horror.

Mr. Beard unfroze first. He looked up, swore loudly, and took a step toward me.

I don't have a weapon, I thought. I can't believe this is how I'll die – at the hands of a madman who thinks he's getting even for a stiletto-stab.

Before I could scream or try to run, Ian leaped onto Mr. Beard's back. Suddenly, Ian had wrapped his arms around Mr. Beard's chest, and his legs around his waist. The next thing I knew, Ian opened his mouth wide, and sank his teeth into the side of Mr. Beard's neck.

"Argh!" Mr. Beard's tiny eyes snapped open wide, round with surprise. His scream was more of annoyance than pain, and he reached back and stabbed Ian in the leg.

I heard myself screaming, as though in the distance. My mind didn't know what was going on, but my body reacted instinctually. I took a few steps forward, and swung my leg up in a high Rockette kick that made firm contact with Mr. Beard's gonads.

He groaned loudly, and bent over at the waist. His grip on the knife loosened, and he pivoted around, trying to shake Ian off his back.

I was thinking about whether I should try to wrestle Mr. Beard's knife away from him, or kick him again, when a familiar voice said, "What's going on here?"

Mr. Beard and Ian froze, and for once, the sight of Detective Elwood made me smile. He was standing in the doorway, pointing his gun at the strange sight of Ian piggybacking on Mr. Beard.

"It's ok, Ian," I said. "You can get off now."

Mr. Beard dropped the knife and Ian released his arms from around Mr. Beard's chest and tried to step back onto the floor. Except he miscalculated how painful his bleeding leg was, slipped, and ended up lying on his back.

"This is my friend, Ian," I told Elwood. "Piggybacking was his way of trying to save me from Mr. Beard here, who was trying to kill me."

I looked at Ian again. He smiled up at me from the floor and I said, "We should get you to the hospital. Your leg looks pretty bad."

"I wanted to talk to you about the burglary," Elwood said, as he handcuffed Mr. Beard and helped Ian stand up. "But I guess you should make a statement about these two freaks, first."

I nodded. "Sorry I didn't get all your messages. I was overseas when you called yesterday."

Elwood shrugged. "No rush. I was just stopping by today to make sure you hadn't left town." I gave him a funny look and he sighed, rolled his eyes and said, "I may have misjudged you."

"It's ok," I said. "I'll drop Ian off at the hospital and come by the station."

"I don't need to go to the hospital," Ian said. "I'm fine. I just bleed a lot." He rolled up his trouser leg to show me. "See?"

I made a face and looked away. "I'm taking you to see a doctor," I told him. "I don't want you to bleed to death right after you saved my life."

THIRTY-FOUR

I drove Ian to the hospital, and the nurse who admitted us took one look at his leg and said he was fine; it was just a slight cut. There'd be a wait, since Ian's situation wasn't critical, so I left him there and went to the police station to make an official statement about Mr. Beard. Elwood told me that Mr. Beard's parole would be revoked, and then I went off to talk to Detective Coles about Crystal's murder.

Three days later, Detective Coles called me up around mid-day. "Sam's DNA matched the DNA found on Crystal's body," he said. "How were you so sure it was him?"

I smiled, allowing myself a moment of pride. "It was the lie," I said. "He wouldn't lie to me if he wasn't hiding something."

"Well," Coles said. "I've got to say, you've got pretty good investigative skills."

The words, "for a casino dealer" seemed to hang in the air, but maybe that was just my imagination.

I called Samantha immediately after that, told her we needed to talk, and drove down to The Peacock Club. I hadn't typed up my report yet, but I wanted to tell her face-to-face what I'd learnt. We grabbed a table in a corner of the half-empty club, and the music pulsed and vibrated around us. I told her, sitting in the semi-dark, what I'd learnt, and she nodded sadly. When I finished, she sniffed and I saw her blink back a tear.

"I should've stopped her," she said. "I should've realized something was up."

"It's not your fault," I said. "She didn't tell anyone what was going on."

We sat silently at the table, and I watched Samantha out of the corner of my eye. She looked slightly silly, dressed in a skimpy pink and white bunny outfit and sky-high pink stilettos, but she was one of those tough women who you wouldn't mind having in your corner. Crystal had been lucky to have her as a friend.

THIRTY-FIVE

Jack and I were sitting in a quiet French restaurant, east of the Strip. It was the kind of place middle-aged men went to meet their mistresses. The words on the menu were unpronounceable, the waiters snooty and condescending, and everything cost too much. But it was dark, out of the way, and the tables were so far from each other that diners could safely talk about things they wouldn't normally discuss in public. For the other diners, this involved a lot of arm-rubbing and coy glances. Jack and I kept our arms to ourselves.

We both ordered the filet mignon, and the waiter sniffed distastefully when I asked for mine to be well done. Jack, of course, was having his medium rare.

We chatted about work, the weather, and our families with the pensiveness of a parent talking with their child's teacher – it was pleasant enough on the surface, but we both knew there was an unpleasant reason for the meeting.

There was no point waiting till dessert to pull out the big guns. So I took a deep breath and told Jack the lie that I'd prepared. "I saw the number plate on the getaway car for the Van Gogh burglary. I ran it through the system; the car's yours."

Jack held my glance for a few seconds. I made sure I looked serious, and confident of what I was saying. Jack's expression was unreadable.

"I know," he said softly.

I tried not to look surprised. I'd expected him to deny the whole thing and a part of me was disappointed that he hadn't given me some excuse, no matter how flimsy – maybe someone had stolen his car, maybe he'd been jumping off the roof of the Ascend for fun that morning.

I looked down at my steak, not caring if my disappointment showed, and sighed.

"I should've told you," Jack said.

"Why?" We looked at each other, and I said, "You could just buy it off Jeremy, and he's your friend. You could've reached a deal."

Jack shook his head. "Money has nothing to do with it. Well, ok. Money has everything to do with it."

Maybe the fillet mignon wasn't agreeing with me. I dabbed my lips with the napkin, and put it down beside my plate.

"Wait," Jack said, just as I was about to push back my chair.

I looked up at his eyes, glistening in the dim lighting, and waited.

"Do you know about Jeremy's son?"

I shook my head. "What's that got to do with anything?"

"Jeremy had health insurance with AAI. But then his son had a snowboarding accident and went into a coma. AAI refused to pay out, and on top of that – they dinged Jeremy's report so he couldn't get health insurance with anyone else."

I looked at Jack, not wanting to believe that a company could be so mean. "What happened to his son?"

Jack looked grimly at his plate. "He's still in a coma, but Jeremy's hoping for the best. A parent never loses hope."

"But the costs are adding up," I suggested, and Jack nodded.

"Jeremy's waiting for some clients to pay him, but he owes money to his suppliers, and he needs to keep paying the hospital bills. So…"

I felt something twist in my stomach, and I rested my head on one hand. "So you thought of this."

"Yes. This'll solve his cash flow problems for a long time."

"He's your friend. Why not just lend him the money?"

Jack smiled, a thin, humorless smile. "And miss the chance to screw with AAI?"

"That's not a very nice attitude."

"It is, if you knew how badly they've treated Jeremy. And at the worst possible time in his life…"

I blinked slowly and looked down at my plate, not feeling good about all this. And yet, I could see what he was getting at – if something were to happen to Nanna, for instance, and the insurance company made things a lot worse, I'd want revenge too.

I sighed. "Why not just have him *give* you the painting?"

Jack shook his head. "That's actually more risky. Getting everything staged and all. Besides, what's the fun in that?"

He was smiling again, but this time his eyes were laughing.

"Why are you telling me?"

Jack shrugged. "Seems like you knew what happened. But not why."

I looked at the half-eaten meal on my plate. I couldn't imagine having another bite, and now I wished I'd waited till after dessert to bring this up.

"I'll have to tell AAI," I said softly.

"You're free to do what you'd like. But now you know about them, and I'll deny whatever I told you."

I looked up at him again. "Then why tell me at all?"

"You keep saying you won't date a criminal. I'm not a criminal."

I smiled thinly. "You just burglarize for fun."

Jack winked. "But let's keep that to ourselves."

"Where's the stolen painting now?"

"I'm keeping it for a few months, and then I'll give it back to Jeremy."

I nodded, and tried to have another bite of my steak as I thought things through.

"Have you done this before?" I asked.

"Burglary? Sure. Whenever things – work, shopping, whatever – get too easy, it's nice to have a challenge."

I pushed the food around on my plate. "I can't eat any more. Will you excuse me?"

Jack signaled for the check, and I waited till he was done paying and could escort me out the door.

Dinner hadn't gone how I'd expected. I didn't know what I *had* expected, but I certainly hadn't expected this.

THIRTY-SIX

I wanted to spend the weekend doing nothing, other than wallowing in my misery. But on Saturday morning, Stone stopped by and dragged me over to the gun range.

"I heard about Mr. Beard attacking you," he said. "You really need to get better at protecting yourself."

He had a point, so I went with him and shot at paper targets for a while. I think I'm improving as a shot, but I it doesn't matter, because I can't carry a gun with me and walk into a casino.

Stone walked over after some time to talk to me, so I took off my earmuffs and looked at him.

"You need to go back to Carla and take more KravMaga lessons," he said.

I winced. Carla was a small, scary woman of indeterminate age and European heritage. She made me punch, kick and otherwise hurt her poor, defenseless assistant. He'd wear some kind of padding, but still. The lessons weren't fun.

"Use it or lose it," Stone said.

"Nanna says that," I told him. "You're turning into Nanna."

He smiled and was about to go back to practice, when I said, "What do you think of Jack?"

"Jack Weber?" He looked at me warily. "He seems ok. Why?"

"I'm thinking of going on a date with him." I held Stone's glance. His eyes were dark and somber, and his expression unreadable.

He took a step forward and pushed a strand of hair behind my right ear. His eyes softened, and for a moment I wondered if he'd lean down and kiss me. But then he stepped back, and his eyes became serious again. "He seems nice enough," he said slowly. "I can't see why not."

And then he went back to his booth, and I put my earmuffs on again.

———

TWO HOURS LATER, Stone and I were sitting in my parents' kitchen, helping ourselves to mashed potatoes. I'd wanted to go straight home from the gun range, but my mother insisted I come over; when Dad heard that Stone was with me, he insisted that Stone come as well.

We were piling up our plates with my mom's cooking, when the front doorbell rang, and my mom jumped up.

"I'll get that," she said, and Nanna and I exchanged a glance.

"It's for you," Nanna told me. "Your mother thinks he's nice."

I rolled my eyes and Stone and Dad ignored the doorbell completely, chatting about some hockey player who'd injured himself, and what the chances were for the team this season, and what the chances were that the guy'd recover from the injury.

My mother walked back into the room with a lanky, curly-haired man following her.

"Tiffany, this is Matt," she told me. "He's having lunch with us."

"Uh, hi everyone," Matt said awkwardly.

Matt had bad skin and wore glasses, and he reminded me of one of the dorks who'd gone to my highschool. Dad and Stone paused their conversation long enough to nod at him, and then they went back to their hockey talk.

"Have a seat," Mom told Matt, pointing to the empty seat beside me, and I did my best not to groan. "Matt's my friend Melanie's son," Mom said. "He teaches history at the local high school."

I looked at him again. Now that she mentioned it, Matt *did* look like a history teacher – he was just the kind of guy you'd throw paper balls at when his back was turned.

"History!" Nanna said. "I reckon I could teach that. Probably better than you."

Mom made a warning sound directed at Nanna, and Matt smiled wanly. I felt kind of sorry for him, but I was more sorry for myself. I looked at Stone, and he glanced at me and winked. "You're on your own," the wink seemed to say.

"Uh," Matt said to me, and then he paused.

Mom, Nanna and I all looked at him, waiting for him to finish his sentence. I thought I saw beads of perspiration on his forehead, and he struggled to come up with another word to say.

"Tiffany's a casino dealer," Mom prompted, trying to help him out, and Matt nodded, and served himself some beans and mashed potatoes to go with his meat.

I decided to ignore him and turned to Nanna. "Where's *your* boyfriend today?"

My mother made a choking noise, and Nanna said, "I didn't know we were having company. If I'd known, I'd asked him to come over. Mr. History here looks like he could use some help with the conversation."

We all looked at him again, and he paused with his fork mid-air, and then put it down.

He turned to me, and took a deep breath. "You're Tiffany," he said.

I felt like the guy wanted some applause, but my sympathy for him was replaced by a sudden irritation. Why did a guy who could barely string two sentences together think I would swoon all over him?

"Yes," I snapped. "And you teach history."

"You're a casino dealer," he said, a hint of condescension in his voice.

"You're right," I replied. "Would you like to get married now?"

I heard the sharp intake of breath coming from my mother's seat, and Nanna said, "You're meant to play hard to get. I know that, which is why I've got myself a boyfriend and you don't."

"I don't want to play hard to get," I told her. "I'm sick of doing things the normal way, and I'm tired of boring people."

Stone and Dad had stopped talking now, and everyone was staring at me.

I turned to Matt, and said, "Let's just get this out of the way, ok? Our parents clearly want us to get to get together. Do you want to be with me? No? Marry me? No? I didn't think so." Matt was staring at me, his jaw dropping almost to his plate.

"I just saved you some time there," I told him. "Now you can go be condescending to some other poor girl."

My mother pinched her lips together and stared at her plate, and Nanna said, "Well, wasn't that a nice idea. Speeding things up. I should do that. After all, I don't have much time left. Maybe thirty years, if I keep up with my water aerobics."

Stone and Dad went back to their conversation, moving from hockey to the NFL now, as though nothing had happened.

Dad's probably given up on me being the good, predictable daughter, and Stone probably thought the conversation had been relatively normal. However, my mother stayed silent and stared at her plate for the rest of the meal, and it was a relief to finally leave.

THIRTY-SEVEN

I stopped by the station on Monday, and Elwood looked up from his coffee mug long enough to glance at me.

"We're dropping the Van Gogh case," he said. "Apparently we've already been on it for too long. Unless you found something you'd like to share with me?"

I shook my head, no. "Figures about the investigation," I said. "The department's strapped for cash, and the guy's painting was insured. Big whoop."

Elwood nodded. "Rich people, huh? Who needs to waste more time helping them?"

I glanced down at Elwood's hands. "No wedding band?"

He smiled proudly. "She agreed to go to counseling with me. But I had to take the band off, first."

———

ONCE I GOT home, I called Jack.

"I'm not working for AAI," I told him, "So who cares what happened to Jeremy's painting? The company sounds like a greedy bunch."

"Does this mean you'll finally go out with me?" Jack said. "On a date?"

"Are there any Harlequin-reading women in your life at the moment?"

There was silence for a few seconds and then Jack said, "Yes." I frowned, but then Jack went on. "My sister. She's the Harlequin-reading one, but she doesn't want people to know. So we say that those books are for my friends."

I smiled, feeling ridiculously happy. "In that case, I suppose a date might be doable."

"I know a lovely Italian place."

I could hear the smile in Jack's voice and I shook my head. "Nope. I don't want some random boring date. I've had it with boring men. I want you to teach me how to break into buildings."

I few seconds went by. I'd expected Jack to say no, but instead, he said, "How about Friday?"

"Perfect. We're on."

If I'd had any idea then just how badly that first date would turn out, I'd have thought twice about saying yes…

If you enjoyed this second book in the Tiffany Black humorous mystery series, make sure you check out Book Three, which will be available in May:

RED ROSES IN LAS VEGAS

Tiffany Black is sick of the dangers that come with being a PI. She's about to throw in the towel, when events force her to investigate one last case…

Nanna is a sweet, lovely old lady – at least, that's what she'd like you to believe. Too bad the cops investigating Adam Bitzer's death don't buy it for a second. And worse, they think she's the one responsible for Adam's death…

ABOUT THE AUTHOR

A.R. Winters loves books, TV series and movies about mysteries, crime capers and heists. She also enjoys a good laugh, so she writes lighthearted, humorous mysteries.

When not writing, she's usually eating too much cake.

CONNECT WITH HER ONLINE:
http://twitter.com/ar_winters
http://www.arwinters.com

JOIN THE A.R. WINTERS NEWSLETTER!

J oin A.R. Winter's newsletter and be the first to hear about her latest book releases, and enjoy exclusive subscriber discounts. You will only ever be contacted if A.R. Winters has a new book out, or if she's running a subscriber-only special or contest.

Go to http://arwinters.com/newsletter to join.

IF YOU ENJOYED READING *GREEN EYES IN LAS VEGAS*,
I WOULD APPRECIATE IT IF YOU WOULD HELP
OTHERS ENJOY THIS BOOK, TOO:

LEND IT. This book is lending-enabled, so please, share it with a friend.

RECOMMEND IT. Please help other readers find this book by recommending it to friends, readers' groups and discussion boards.

REVIEW IT. Please tell other readers why you liked this book by reviewing it at Amazon or Goodreads. If you do write a review, please send me an email at arwintersfiction@gmail.com so I can thank you personally, or visit me at http://www.arwinters.com.

66713579R00148

Made in the USA
Columbia, SC
19 July 2019